"Let's practice some more." Chance offered Caro his hand.

She nodded, her blond hair falling over one shoulder as she took his hand. He pulled her to her feet. In a moment she was up against him again.

Damn.

If she had any idea how it tortured him to have her back up against him like she was, well, suffice it to say, she'd probably call off the rest of their self-defense lesson.

"Remember," he said into her ear. "Step, wedge, thrust."

He didn't give her time to comment, just wrapped an arm around her. She didn't hesitate this time, shoving her leg between his own, thrusting back, using such force that he didn't have to fake falling down.

He loved the way her eyes lit up with triumph.

"That was easy." She grinned.

"Let's do it again."

It was all he could do not to lean down and plant his lips on hers.

Dear Reader,

Many years ago I decided to try trick riding. Problem was, I didn't own a horse. No matter. The local rancher had a few trusty steeds and so I figured I'd ride one of them. Using a giant oak tree as a perch, I waited patiently for a horse to wander beneath me. When the moment was right, I flung myself atop the horse's back.

I rode for about 1.9 seconds.

Actually, I bounced...and bounced...ever closer toward the rear, and then I catapulted into the air. I did not, however, bounce when I hit the ground. I ached for days.

It was worth it.

That moment fueled a lifelong passion for horses. I never did make it into the trick riding arena, but I am proud to call a few of those riders my friends. Every time I watch them perform, I am left breathless. I hoped to capture that breathlessness in *The Ranger's Rodeo Rebel*.

Trick riders are tough. My heroine, Carolina Cruthers, is tough, too, but not when it comes to relationships. My hero, Chance Reynolds, is exactly the kind of man she tries to avoid: bossy, bold and just a tad bit too handsome for his own good. Fate draws them together and forces Chance to act as Carolina's bodyguard. Together they learn that sometimes even the strongest individuals need a little help.

I hope you enjoy *The Ranger's Rodeo Rebel*. As always, it is my fondest hope that readers will laugh and cry when they read my books. I hope I've succeeded.

Pam

THE RANGER'S RODEO REBEL

PAMELA BRITTON

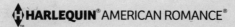
HARLEQUIN® AMERICAN ROMANCE®

Recycling programs
for this product may
not exist in your area.

ISBN-13: 978-0-373-75623-0

The Ranger's Rodeo Rebel

Copyright © 2016 by Pamela Britton

Printed in U.S.A.

With more than a million books in print, **Pamela Britton** likes to call herself the best-known author nobody's ever heard of. Of course, that changed thanks to a certain licensing agreement with that little racing organization known as NASCAR.

But before the glitz and glamour of NASCAR, Pamela wrote books that were frequently voted the best of the best by the *Detroit Free Press*, Barnes & Noble (two years in a row) and *RT Book Reviews*. She's won numerous awards, including a National Readers' Choice Award and a nomination for the Romance Writers of America Golden Heart® Award.

When not writing books, Pamela is a reporter for a local newspaper. She's also a columnist for the *American Quarter Horse Journal*.

Books by Pamela Britton

Harlequin American Romance

The Cowgirl's CEO
The Wrangler
Mark: Secret Cowboy
Rancher and Protector
The Rancher's Bride
A Cowboy's Pride
A Cowboy's Christmas Wedding
A Cowboy's Angel
The Texan's Twins
Kissed by a Cowboy
Her Rodeo Hero
His Rodeo Sweetheart

Visit the Author Profile page
at Harlequin.com for more titles.

For Josey Lynn and Bobbie Stone, two of the most amazing trick riders in the rodeo business, and women I'm proud to call my friends.

Chapter One

It had turned into the day from hell.

"Come on." Carolina Cruthers patted the pockets of her jeans one last time. "Please tell me I didn't do what I think I did."

But her denim pants didn't hold the keys to her truck any more than her hands did, which meant she'd either lost them in the barn or they were somewhere inside her truck.

Dang it. She peered quickly around the parking area of Misfit Farms, her blond braids nearly slapping her in the face. The bright afternoon sun turned the farm's newly installed fence the same color as the new cars on Via Del Caballo's main drag: pristine white.

In truth, Carolina had no idea why she bothered to look around. She knew she'd dropped her keys somewhere in her truck. She'd done it enough times the past month it was a sure bet. Nobody would come to her rescue, either. Today was Monday. Misfit Farms was closed to clients and visitors. This was the day when she and her boss, Colt Reynolds, reviewed rodeo business. They had talked about their specialty act this morning, the upcoming schedule and any changes they needed to make after their weekend performance. Her boss had left earlier along with his wife, Natalie. There was nobody walking around the state-of-the-art horse facility.

Now what? She cupped her hands and peered through the truck's window. Her keys weren't in the ignition, so they were most likely—

On the floor.

Yep. Just beneath the edge of the driver's seat, glinting in the sun, sat the horseshoe charm Colt and Natalie had gotten her for Christmas. The charm lay on the black mat of her truck as if making fun of her dilemma. Lucky. Yeah, right.

She'd done it again. She'd locked her stupid keys in her dang truck. This was…what? The third time in the past month? And all because of…

James.

The reason for her absentmindedness settled into the pit of her stomach like a load of cement. She probably had a million texts on her phone right now, the same cell phone tucked inside her purse, the one resting on the bench seat in the rear of her vehicle.

Think.

She picked up a braid and absently started chewing—a habit of hers. Colt and Natalie wouldn't be back for at least an hour. That meant it was just her with no cell phone and no access to a landline unless the barn office was open or she broke into her boss's house. If that was the case, there was a phone upstairs in the abandoned apartment above the barn. Abandoned…but not for long.

That had been the other piece of news that had rattled her. Her boss had decided to stay home the rest of the season. Colt was putting his brother in charge of their rodeo specialty act. Chance Reynolds was the guy's name. A man who'd been out of the business for years.

And yet Colt thought he'd be better suited to take over. Not fair. She'd been around longer. She'd put in years of blood, sweat and tears, not with Colt and the Galloping Girlz, but with another team. She'd even taken over when her friend Samantha had decided to run off with her movie-star boyfriend. Why Colt had decided to put some former Army Ranger in charge was beyond her, but it had seriously bummed her out.

Keys, she reminded herself. She wouldn't be able to go home and sulk unless she found her keys.

The walk to the main barn was a short one. The horses in the stalls hung their heads out to greet her. Hanoverians, Trakehners and other imported warm bloods mixed with the occasional Thoroughbred. They peeked at her curiously, ears pricked forward as if asking, "Food?"

"Not yet, guys," she said.

Carolina kind of understood why Colt had decided to sit out the rest of the rodeo season. His wife, Natalie, a famous hunter/jumper rider, with a waiting list of people wanting to train with her, was about to have a baby. The doctor had recently grounded her. Colt wanted to be around to help with the baby when it came. Someone needed to keep riding all the horses, and that was Colt. Carolina didn't blame him. She just couldn't stand the idea of some flatlander telling her what to do. It made no sense.

At the far end of the barn, near a patch of sunlight that nearly blinded her, was the office, its fancy French doors closed. She said a silent prayer heavenward and turned the handle.

It didn't move.

She rattled it some more, just in case, jiggling the door so hard dust fell from the sill above. The door wouldn't

budge. Okay, fine. Up to the apartment she would go.
No big deal. When she got home she'd pour herself a big
glass of wine. Maybe even take a bath. It'd been forever
since she'd had one of those.

The stairs to the apartment were outside at the back of
the barn. It was a steep climb that had her heart thumping from the exertion of taking the steps two at a time,
but her reward was a door handle that slid down easily.
Carolina released a breath of relief and all but dived for
the phone.

A man stood in front of her.

A tall man with black hair and green eyes and a face
that resembled her boss so much she knew in an instant
who he was.

Chance Reynolds.

And he was naked.

HE SHOULD MOVE, Chance thought, standing in the living
area of his new home. He should, but he couldn't seem
to make himself, because there was something so incredibly priceless about the look on the woman's face.

"Oh, my goodness, I'm so—"

The rest of what she'd been about to say was lost in
her mad scramble to run away.

You would have thought he was naked. As he glanced
down at himself he admitted she probably thought exactly that. He wore military-issue underwear that happened to be the same color as desert sand. In other
words: nude.

"Hey, wait," he shouted. He grabbed the jeans he'd
thrown over the back of the small couch.

"Really." He ran and tugged, ran and tugged, hopping
and skipping as he headed for the door. The woman was

already at the bottom of the steps by the time he poked his head outside, his pants still open at the zipper. "Stop."

She paused with her hand still on the rail. "I'd like to borrow your phone," she said without making eye contact.

"Hold on." He zipped up his jeans and glanced back inside his apartment for a shirt. He'd been extremely sleep deprived when his brother had dropped him off at three this morning, and he wasn't sure where anything was. His bag sat by the door, but he saw no sign of his shirt, not even on the floor of the tiny kitchen to the left of the door.

"Seriously," he called. "Come back up. I'm dressed."

She slowly faced him, her eyes looking anywhere but at him. When she peeked up and noticed he was shirt-less, she immediately glanced away, her face turning red.

He laughed. "All right, I'm half-dressed."

"I just need to use the phone," she repeated.

"Feel free." The woman with twin blond braids took a deep breath, apparently weighing her options. Chance didn't mind. It gave him the opportunity to study her. She was slight of build and wearing jeans and a black shirt that hugged her curves and displayed the narrow width of her waist. He had a pretty good idea who she was. Carolina Cruthers. He'd seen her picture on his brother's website. Trick rider. His new employee.

She must have made up her mind, because she slowly climbed the stairs, her boots clunking up the wooden steps, the sound echoing off the roof of the covered arena a few dozen feet away.

"Need to call a tow company," she muttered on her way by.

He swung the door closed behind her. "If you're having car problems, I can take a look."

"No, thanks." She'd clearly been to the apartment before, because she walked straight to the phone in the kitchen.

"Thanks." She turned away from him, dialed a number. "Hi," he heard her all but whisper into the white handset. Curious, he followed her. Her gaze met his and she half turned away. "This is Carolina Cruthers. I—" She slapped her mouth closed and, judging by the way her full lips pressed together, she wasn't happy about what someone said on the other end. "Actually, yes, I did." She lowered her voice even more. "I'm at work." She gave an address, one he instantly recognized as his own. Well, it'd been his when he was a kid, growing up on Reynolds Ranch. He still owned fifty-plus acres to the east, part of his inheritance when his dad died. One day he would build there, but for now, he was ensconced in his brother's fancy barn.

"I'll be waiting." She hung up, lifted a hand in apology. "Sorry to bug you."

"How long before they get here?"

Her eyes dipped down, but not before he spotted the way they lingered on his chest. He supposed he should feel self-conscious standing in front of her half-naked, but he hadn't spent the last eight years of his life in the military, four of them as an Army Ranger, without learning how to be comfortable in his own skin.

"Half hour, they said. Maybe more."

"Locked your keys in your truck again?"

Her eyes widened in surprise, and he caught his first good look at their color. Light blue. The color of the sky first thing in the morning. The ring around the pupils so dark it made the lightness stand out. Some men might find her twin braids, worn jeans and dirty boots attractive, but he liked his women far more feminine.

"I guess Colt told you about me."

He'd been told the woman had been through a lot. He scanned her arms and her face. No sign of the bruises his brother had mentioned. He *did* notice, though, that for someone who tried to project toughness, she had a very fragile-looking face. Tiny chin. Small nose. High cheekbones, and skin as pale as the fresh snow that sometimes fell in the desert.

"He told me you were in a spot of trouble."

"That's one way of putting it," she said before tipping her chin up. "Thanks for letting me use your phone. I'll wait outside."

"No need." He spotted his shirt on the floor near the couch, up next to the wall. He must have shed his clothes on his way to bed. "Sit down and relax."

The words brought to mind a different image, one that had no business slipping into his thoughts, especially given what she'd just been through. *Especially* given where he'd just come from. Behind enemy lines. Fighting insurgents. Trying to survive. He still couldn't quite grasp he was home again.

Home to babysit the woman in front of him.

Because that's what it boiled down to. Truth was, his brother had been worried about his rodeo trick rider. Really worried. Concerned enough that he'd put Chance in charge of the rodeo act. Carolina had been acting funny, too, Colt had told him. Like locking her keys in her truck and forgetting portions of her routine. His brother had a feeling there was more to the breakup with her ex than she let on. He was pretty sure she was being stalked, not that she'd tell anyone anything. Typical cowgirl. They thought they could handle anything without a man's help.

"Thanks, but that's okay." She took a deep breath, and though she was tiny, she tried to make herself look ten feet tall by standing up straight. "I can wait outside." She turned to leave.

He cleared his throat. "I bet I can open the door of your truck long before a tow service gets here."

She paused with her hand on the door. "No, you can't."

"Yes, I can." Breaking into vehicles had been part of his military training. That, and a few other things she didn't need to know about. "Sixty seconds, maybe less."

"You think?"

"Just give me a knife."

"A knife?"

"That's all I need."

She didn't look convinced. "There's some utensils in the kitchen drawers, I think, if you really want to give it a try."

Try? Army Rangers didn't just try. They *did*.

He moved forward. "Chance Reynolds."

She wiped her palms on the front of her jeans before saying, "Carolina Cruthers." She shook his hand.

She couldn't take her eyes off his chest, and the sight of her blushing, embarrassed and so clearly uncomfortable, gave him an odd sort of pleasure. It shouldn't. He wasn't back in the States to get involved with anyone. In a short time, he'd be back over there—the Middle East again—as a private contractor. Besides, relationships with cowgirls weren't his thing. He'd gone that route before, during his high school rodeoing days, but they were too independent for their own good. Drove him nuts.

"I'll meet you downstairs." She backed away, spun and exited the door like a horse bolting for the barn, which he supposed in a way she was.

Carolina Cruthers.

He tasted the name on his lips. She wasn't what he'd expected at all. The Carolina from the website had looked pretty enough, but he'd figured she'd be loud and crass and obnoxious. A cowgirl in overalls, a cowboy hat and with a piece of straw hanging out of her mouth. This Carolina was shy and innocent and, yes, *pretty*.

And as he listened to her feet fly down the steps, he couldn't decide if that was a good thing…or bad.

Chapter Two

Please let him find a shirt. Please let him find a shirt. Pleasepleasepleaseplease.

"You ready?"

She jumped.

He stared at her with concern. "Easy there, sparky." He smiled, his big strong jaw with its ridge of muscle along the bottom jutting out. "You'll give yourself a heart attack."

He wore a shirt. Thank God he wore a shirt. But for some reason, the sight of him with clothes on wasn't any better than the sight of him half-naked. Damn that Colt Reynolds. Why hadn't he told her he'd come home? Then again, maybe he had. Maybe she'd been so distracted by James's latest text she'd missed that tiny tidbit of information. It wouldn't surprise her. Not that it mattered. Nothing could have prepared her for the sight of Chance Reynolds in the flesh. Something about the man made her want to melt into the ground. Maybe it was his eyes. Or maybe it was his height and the way his bearing and short hair had the stamp of a military man. He was taller than Colt. His face was shaped differently, too. Chance was one of those guys who could easily be in films, with his sweeping brows and thick lower lip. He had scruff on his chin, too, and along the ridge of his jaw, a stain of color that turned his tan skin a darker brown. She'd taken one look at him and turned as stupidly speechless as a starstruck teen.

"Sorry." She forced a smile. "I'm a little jumpy today."

He gave her a look that she didn't quite understand, maybe because she had turned away too quickly. It had almost seemed like sympathy, although he had no reason to feel sorry for her…unless. Goodness, he didn't know about James, did he?

"Here." He headed toward her truck, holding what looked like a butter knife in his right hand. "Let's get you squared away."

He did know. Of course Colt had told him. Why wouldn't he? One of his employees had come to him battered, bruised and scared. The cops had been called. James had been arrested. Any responsible employer would share that news with a new employee.

Not an employee. His brother.

Whatever. But Colt didn't know about the threats that had been coming more and more steadily in recent weeks. She'd told no one about those except for law enforcement and her social worker. Having a boyfriend beat her within an inch of her life was enough. No wonder Chance looked at her so sadly.

She *was* sad.

Click.

The sound startled her. Chance had opened her truck door, and she had no clue how he'd done it.

"That's incredible," she said.

Movie-star man simply smiled. "You should see what I can do with a spoon." He grinned, tossed the knife into the air and caught it by the handle like a ninja warrior.

That's what he looked like, his arms huge, muscled and toned. His chest had been pretty spectacular, too. He had a deep ridge between his two pectoral muscles, and beneath that, square-shaped mounds, each one smaller than the other. His skin had looked as soft as lambskin, and so toned and hard she'd flushed like a piece of fruit in the summer sun when she'd spotted him standing at the top of those stairs. She'd never had a reaction like that to a man before. Never.

Movie-star man stared at her oddly.

"Th-thank you so much," she stammered. And now she couldn't even talk right.

"You're welcome."

She hated that she found him attractive. She would be working with him. That should have made her feel depressed, not...titillated.

"I should call the tow company," she said, shuffling past him, pulling her truck door open and reaching for her purse. Sad that she had the tow company's phone number memorized. She grabbed her phone...and saw it.

Twenty missed calls. Thirty text messages.

Oh, dear Lord.

"What's wrong?"

"Nothing."

She couldn't tell him what was wrong. This man was her new boss. The last thing she needed was to give him a bad impression by admitting how messed-up her life was.

"Is he stalking you?"

So he *did* know about James.

His eyes said it all. *I know enough.*

"Is he?"

She wanted to crumble. It made her so angry she

fought back tears. She was *not* that woman, the one from some reality TV show who allowed a man to beat her and terrorize her and then crumbled at another man's feet. She was strong. She could handle this. She could.

She was *not* her mom.

"Let me see your phone."

She didn't want him to look, and that killed her all over again, so much so when he reached for the phone she didn't try to keep it away from him. It fell limply into his grasp.

"Wow." He looked up from the screen. "Have you read these?"

She shook her head. What could she say? That she'd been too scared, and that had upset her all over again. How had it happened? How had she turned into such a complete loser? How had she followed in her mother's footsteps?

James, she admitted. He'd beaten the confidence out of her.

"We're calling the cops."

"I called them already. Yesterday." At least she'd found her voice again.

"And what did they say?"

"That they'd done everything they could. They talked to him. Warned him. I've filed for an emergency restraining order, but it's not doing any good. He..." She swallowed. Why was this so hard to admit? "Follows me."

He might even be outside the gates of Misfit Farms right now. He had been before.

"I'm taking you home."

She straightened. "No. I can handle my ex."

His expression was firm and implacable. "You don't have a choice."

"And you don't have a vehicle." She hadn't seen one other than Colt's big pickup truck.

"Colt said I could use his."

"But then I'd have to leave my truck here."

"I'll take you wherever you need to go from here on out."

"That's too much." She took a deep breath and repeated, "I can handle this."

She could handle a fifteen-hundred-pound horse. Do tricks on them nobody in their right mind wanted to try. James was a scrawny human who liked to terrorize little women. She would deal.

"Look," he said. "I wanted Colt to tell you this, but he was afraid you'd think he'd overstepped his bounds. Plus, I think he wanted to spare you the embarrassment."

She tensed.

"The truth is, I'm not just your boss."

She couldn't move. She had a feeling she wouldn't like what came next.

"I'm your bodyguard."

She blinked. "Excuse me?"

"You're the reason why Colt put me in charge of his specialty act. Well, that and the fact my sister-in-law is pregnant and Colt plans to stay home with her soon. But while I learn the ropes, he's asked me to keep an eye on you, and if you don't mind, I'm going to do exactly that. Stay here. I'll be right back with my brother's truck."

She shook her head, attempted to catch his sleeve, but he was already gone.

I'm your bodyguard.

Dear Lord in heaven.

Her humiliation was now complete.

"You really don't have to do this," Carolina said, smoothing down her blond pigtails.

"Actually, I do."

His brother had filled him in on the situation last night. Told him about his idea, too, to put him in charge. It'd seemed stupid at first. He hadn't ridden a horse in years, but Colt had insisted. The act didn't involve riding, at least not on his part. It was all tricks from the ground, done by sleight of hand and verbal commands. The Galloping Girlz did the actual riding. All he'd have to do was learn the routine and keep an eye on the woman standing in front of him. A little woman. Someone easy to terrorize, by the looks of things.

"Where to?" he asked.

She didn't seem happy, but when he opened the passenger-side door, she climbed in. "Do you know where the rodeo grounds are?"

"I think I do." It'd been eight years, but he was pretty sure he could still find his way around.

"I live about a mile from them."

Clear across town. Well, so be it. Those hadn't been mild threats on her phone. They'd been a stream of vitriol so nasty he didn't blame her for being distressed. If he'd had someone threatening to do those things, he'd be a little distracted, too.

"How long did you date this guy?"

She'd settled into her seat. "About a year."

"Long time," he observed, backing out of Colt's parking spot next to a massive six-horse trailer with the name *Rodeo Misfits* on the side.

"Too long," she added.

He cocked an eyebrow at her in question.

"I wanted to break up months ago, but I was…" She licked her lips.

"Scared," he finished for her.

She nodded. "Turns out, I'm not the only woman he's done this to. I felt like such an idiot when I heard that."

He was about to put the truck in Drive, but something in her eyes stopped him. She had the air of a woman who'd seen something terrible, something she didn't want to see again but that still haunted her soul.

He drummed his fingers on the steering wheel. "You know, maybe you should move into the apartment above the barn. Just temporarily. Colt said I could have it, but I can bunk down with Colt or at my sister's place down the road."

She sat up in her seat. "No. I can't do that."

But the more he thought about it, the more he liked the idea. He didn't know the woman next to him, not really. His brother had told him a lot. City girl who'd grown up with a love for horses. She'd found trick riding relatively late in life: sixteen. She was twenty-six now, and his brother said she was good, doing tricks he'd never seen before.

Brave.

But not at this moment. He felt a keen sense of protectiveness. The same kind of urge he'd felt when he'd stumbled into a village of Afghans, scared, dragged into a war they didn't want, kids crying, women terrified. Tore him apart. The urge to shield them and keep them from harm was one he had never ignored.

"Ready?" She met his gaze, peering up at him with an unblinking stare. "You can take me home. Nothing will happen, I promise. I can handle this on my own. Don't make this a bigger deal than it already is."

Because then you'll give my ex the power. He read the words in her eyes. He understood that look, too. When he'd been fighting over there, he'd seen the same expression of resolve. They didn't want the US military's help. They wanted to be left alone to deal with things on their own. They wanted independence.

He couldn't blame her for that.

"As long as you think you have it handled," he said.

"I do."

He nodded, and she faced forward again, so clearly relieved he couldn't help but feel a twinge of admiration for her as he put his brother's truck in gear and drove toward her home.

"Colt told me you'll only be Stateside for a short time?"

He appreciated her attempt at conversation. For some reason, sitting next to her made him antsy. "Going to work for DTS—Darkhorse Tactical Solutions. Just taking a sabbatical while my sister-in-law finishes cooking her baby."

She smiled. That was better. He liked that smile. It tipped the end of her nose up and made the corners of her eyes wrinkle. Pretty eyes. Blue as the desert sky on a winter morning.

"What will you be doing for them?" she asked.

"Typical contract work." He glanced at her as he passed between the white fencing his sister-in-law insisted was de rigueur for the ranch. He had to admit, the place looked spectacular. When he'd first driven up, he'd been blown away by the changes made since his brother's wedding. Huge barn. Covered arena. Irrigated pasture. Turned out, they'd been sitting on a gold mine and never known it—a natural aquifer supplied water to the ranch, as well as a few neighbors, for a price.

"I've always wondered what a military contractor does." She smiled again. "I assume you're not building houses."

He shook his head. "We're a security service. Mostly corporate executives, although we do escort the occasional civvy. Our job is to keep someone safe while they do business in war-torn towns."

A blond brow arched. "Business? When there's a war going on?"

"Yup. Sometimes it's military business, sometimes it's civilian business. The need for oil never stops, and billion-dollar corporations need protection for the people who work to bring the product to market. Plus there's road reconstruction companies and real estate investors—"

"You're kidding."

"Nope. War or no, life goes on."

She lapsed into silence, and he let her contemplate his words. A lot of people had no idea what it was really like in the Middle East. All they saw were the bits on TV. Five minutes of chaos followed by days, sometimes weeks, of normalcy. Well, as normal as life in a war-torn country could be. In those moments, people tried to get on with their lives, businesses tried to regroup and recoup. It wasn't as if life stopped. The corporate machine kept moving.

"This is it," she said, interrupting his thoughts. "Turn here."

He followed her directions, turning down a street with two-story apartment complexes on both sides.

"Thank you," she said as he pulled up in front of her building.

"Not so fast." He shut off the engine. "I'm walking you to your door."

She shook her head, the twin braids sliding behind her shoulders. "There's no need. He's not there. If he was, we'd see his truck parked down the road."

"Has he done that before?"

He saw her eyes flicker. "Not lately."

He had a feeling that "not lately" meant not within the last few days. She might be putting on a brave face, but her eyes conveyed the pictures in her mind.

"I'm still walking you to your door," he said, slipping out of the truck. "And I'll be by tomorrow to pick you up around ten."

Her forehead wrinkled as though she wanted to argue, but she nodded just the same and then slid out of the vehicle. She walked ahead of him as she crossed the tiny grass hill separating the road from the apartment complex.

"I'm the second one on the left," she explained. "Bottom floor."

Which was why they didn't see it at first.

BITCH.

She stopped in her tracks. He did, too. Her front door had been shielded from their view by her neighbor's tiny porch, the word that'd been spray painted in red only visible from a certain angle.

"Son of a—" She didn't finish what she wanted to say, but there was no need. She froze, eyes wide, hands clenching and unclenching in…what emotion did he see on her face? Dismay? Disgust? Rage? Maybe a combination of it all.

"You're staying with me," he said firmly.

"Yes." She turned to face him, and to his surprise, tears glinted in her eyes. The sight kicked him in the gut. "And I'll stay at the ranch, too, if you don't mind."

Chapter Three

There was something completely mortifying about having to accept the help of a near stranger. Worse, she'd had to call her boss and tell him what had happened. Colt Reynolds had been completely kind, but then again, he always was. She'd never met someone with such a huge capacity to help people in need. In hindsight, it should be no surprise that his little brother was the same way.

Well, there was nothing *little* about him.

"You really don't have to move in with your brother, though," Carolina said, glancing behind them to make sure no silver 4x4 followed. So far, so good. No sign of James. "I can stay in my horse trailer. I do it all the time."

"Does it have living quarters?"

"Well, no." Not technically. She'd never been able to afford one of those big fancy trailers. Her own humble stock trailer was all she had in the world. That and her truck. "I converted the tack room into a space where I could sleep. It has a bed over the hitch and electricity for a portable stove. It works fine."

"Does it have a bathroom?"

"Well, no—"

"A heater or air-conditioning?"

"No, but maybe I could live in the Galloping Girlz

trailer? It has living quarters." She paused. "Or maybe I can stay in Colt's trailer?" Her boss had her dream trailer. Shower. Kitchen. Living area.

One day.

"Maybe, but we'll need to use it on the weekends for rodeos." He stared at her. "What are you doing to do? Move in and out every weekend? And before you suggest it, the trick-riding rig is out, too. There's a perfectly good apartment at the ranch. You're going to stay there and I'll move in with my sister or brother. Capisce?"

She didn't want to, but she nodded just the same. Carolina glanced at the neighborhoods they passed, her mind settling on one word: rodeo. James would follow her to one of them. She would stake her life on it, and there would be no way to avoid the man—not in a public place. Her stomach curdled thinking about it.

They passed the burger joint outside town, and she caught sight of a young couple facing each other in the gravel parking lot. The girl sat on the tailgate, a look of love on her face as she gazed into the eyes of the captain of the high school football team.

Okay, she had no way of knowing if that were true. Carolina looked away from the scene because it made her think of her own childhood. Had she ever really had one? There'd never been time to date anybody, much less a football player. She'd been too busy working two jobs and trying to graduate. She'd refused to flunk out like her mother. Carolina had been determined to do things differently, but look what it'd gotten her. The first man she ever dated had ended up being a complete psycho— just like the men her mom used to bring home. It was enough to put her off men for the rest of her life.

"I'll move back into my old room at Colt's," Chance

said, drawing her attention. "I don't think they've completely babied it out. And they won't mind, not once we explain the situation."

Oh, yeah, sure. Explain that Carolina's ex-boyfriend was even crazier than she'd thought. Great.

Do not start crying.

She inhaled sharply. Tears were for babies. She wasn't one and she wouldn't act like one, either. So what if she was in a spot of trouble with her ex? She'd deal with it. And she had help, she thought, glancing at her companion in the truck. Chance was much younger than her boss, at least five years, but clearly older than her. And while her boss was a handsome older man, Chance Reynolds wasn't handsome. The former Army Ranger was drop-dead gorgeous. Like Tatum Channing, only with a way better body. She should know. She'd seen the whole enchilada.

Carolina!

"Have you lived here long?" he asked.

"My whole life." She'd known who the Reynoldses were long before they'd known her. Their father was legendary in rodeo circles. A member of the Hall of Fame, a world-renowned horse trainer. She'd heard about the dark side of Zeke Reynolds, too. His infamous temper. His ghastly horse-training techniques. Even that he might have beaten the boys and their sister. She'd seen no evidence of it, though. Her boss never spoke ill of his dad, and when she'd brought Zeke Reynolds up one day, all Colt had done was shrug and repeat what Carolina thought—the man had been a legend.

"You go to the local high school?" Chance asked.

The only high school. "Via Del Caballo High."

"Go, Chargers," Colt sang.

She smiled. A rearing horse was the school's mascot, and it was the reason why she'd gotten into horses, much to her mother's dismay. Carolina had always been fascinated by them, but when one of the local cowboys had brought his horse to the football game her freshman year—in a foil and cardboard costume made to look like armor, of course—she'd been able to touch one for the first time. It'd been over for her ever since. Once she'd looked into those liquid brown eyes, her life had changed.

"You graduated a few years ahead of me," she said. "I remember your sister, Claire. She graduated my freshman year. She always seemed nice."

"My sister is the best," Chance said. "Kills me what she's been through."

Cancer. Not Claire, her son. Leukemia. But they had it on the run, she'd heard.

"You'd never know there was anything amiss from meeting her."

Claire Reynolds was her hero. A woman she could look up to, and she did. Natalie Reynolds, too. Natalie had been in a horrible riding accident before she'd met Colt. They'd told her she'd never walk again, and now look. By comparison, Carolina's problems seemed small.

"Everyone has a cross to bear," he said softly.

She gulped at the kindness and understanding in his eyes. She forced her gaze away and out the window. They were out in what Carolina used to call the boondocks back when she was growing up. The town of Via Del Caballo had faded into tiny ranches—or wannabe ranches, as Carolina called them—single-story houses surrounded by white fences and small arenas. She glanced behind them again. Still no 4x4 in sight.

"We're not being followed," Chance said.

She jerked around so fast her braids nearly hit her in the face. "How do you know?"

"Simple." He glanced at her quickly, the line of his jaw so strong and masculine she swallowed. "I doubled back when we were in town."

He had? Good heavens. She hadn't even noticed.

"You should get in the habit of that, too," he said in a matter-of-fact tone of voice. "Pick a street you know isn't a dead end, one that will allow you to double back. If someone's following you, they'll take the same route, and you'll know it's a bad guy, because nobody's going to do circles for no reason."

She nodded.

"And don't assume he'll be in his truck, either."

She glanced at him sharply, because that's exactly what she'd been looking for.

"He could change vehicles." He rested his wrist on the top of the steering wheel in a manner of complete ease. She supposed compared to driving in a war zone, her situation must seem like Disneyland to him. "And if you are being followed, don't let on that you know. The worst thing you can do is speed up and try and outrun him."

"What do I do?"

"Call 911. Or me. Head to the police station. The man's not going to follow you there. Not unless he's stupid."

She hadn't really thought about that. Yipes.

"If you aren't paying attention," Chance continued, "and you notice he's followed you to the ranch, don't worry too much. Just come on inside. He's not going to come down our road, and if he does, I'll take care of him."

"What about Natalie's clients? Or Claire's? What if he somehow sneaks in thanks to them? What if he hides out or waits until I'm alone?"

Claire ran a canine rescue not far from where Colt lived. Natalie ran a successful horse-jumping business. There was no telling who might accidentally let James in—if it came to that. Carolina doubted he'd come after her like that, though. He was simply mad she'd turned him in. It made him feel like a big man to terrorize her. He was succeeding, and that made her angry all over again. No man should ever have that kind of power over a woman.

"I'll have Claire call her clients tonight and explain what's going on."

Oh, great.

"I'll ask Natalie to take precautions with her clients, too."

So the whole family would now know what an idiot ex-boyfriend she had. Terrific.

BITCH.

Her skin prickled as she recalled the red color. She never would have thought he'd go that far. Now that some of the shock had faded, it made her furious. How dare he deface her property? Granted, it was just a tiny apartment, but she'd worked hard to get the place, and now her landlord would likely throw a fit—and she'd have to pay to fix it, too.

"It'll be okay," Chance said, patting her leg, which made her madder, because she wasn't some little girl who needed a pat on the head—or the leg, as the case might be. She was a full-on adult who could take care of herself.

Then why are you glad a former Army Ranger is sitting next to you? And why are you grateful he'll be with you tonight? And why does the sight of his hand on your leg make you all squirmy inside?

They were questions she refused to answer.

PRICKLY.

That was the word he would use to describe her. Chance pulled his brother's black truck into its parking space and added the word to his list of *stubborn, fiercely independent* and *dogged.*

"Looks like your brother's back," Carolina said.

Colt and Natalie had matching trucks, except for their different colors, and they'd clearly returned from running errands. Chance hadn't heard them leave this morning, which just went to show how completely wiped he'd been from his long journey home. It'd been an eight-hour hitch to Europe, then another eight across the pond. A quick stop on the East Coast, where he'd managed to snatch a nap in an empty hangar only to be headed out again less than an hour later. All told, he'd traveled for twenty-four hours. He'd gone straight to bed once he'd arrived home. Not that it'd helped. He was still bone tired.

"I'll go in and talk to him," he said.

"No. That's okay. I can explain the situation."

Yup. Independent.

He shook his head. "We'll go in together."

It was strange walking up to the house he'd grown up in. Strange and unsettling, in a way. Saying he'd had a bad childhood was like saying Abraham Lincoln had a bad night at the theater. His father had terrified all three of his kids, but he'd taken out his temper on Colt the most. His brother used to say their dad tried out his evil tricks on him first, then used them on Chance or Claire. As they'd gotten older, they'd gotten wiser, especially Colt. He'd taken to preempting their dad, but not always. There'd been times when none of them had been able to avoid the drunken fits.

And so as Chance turned the handle to the front door, he braced himself. He hadn't been inside since his brother's wedding, not even when he'd returned home last night, and he really wasn't sure what to expect.

"Anyone home?" he called, though he knew there was. He took two steps and then stopped.

Where before there'd been a small sitting room and a room beyond, there was now open space. The wall he'd been thrown against as a twelve-year-old—after he'd dared to tell his dad he was too sick to walk to school—had been removed. The kitchen was still to his right, but the wall separating it from the sitting room had been removed. The whole first floor was open, and it felt so different that he instantly relaxed.

"We're up here," a female voice called. His sister-in-law, Natalie. "In your old room."

He caught Carolina's eye. She couldn't seem to stop her gaze from moving around the room, as if she were in awe of the scope of the place, and maybe even a little intimidated.

"I'll stay down here," she said.

"No. Come up. I'm sure they won't mind."

He glanced around again. It was like a whole new home.

Maybe that was the point.

He glanced at Carolina. She clearly didn't want to

go, but he touched her shoulder and urged her forward. He could feel the tension beneath his hand as they headed toward the stairs on the left. The staircase was the one thing that hadn't changed. The oak banister he'd tried to slide down still existed. His father used to make them march up those stairs when they'd been bad. Chance remembered looking up at the top landing, heart pounding...

Enough.

That was in the past. He was a different person. Not the frightened child who'd grown up with an abusive father. And this was a different house. Pictures of Natalie jumping the most amazing horses hung on the stairwell wall. Pictures of his brother, too, at rodeos and reining competitions. Pictures of Natalie's protégée, Laney, in the winner's circle. And in the middle of it all, a picture of the three of them, Colt, Claire and Chance, blown up big, and smiling. He was young. His mom held him in her lap, which meant his dad must have taken the picture.

"Is that you?" Carolina asked.

He jerked his gaze away from the image. "Yup." He tapped the picture. "And Claire and Colt." Not that anyone would need to be told. They all had dark hair. Only the eyes were different. Colt's were hazel, Claire's and his own eyes were green.

"You were so young," she observed.

"Yes, we were."

There had been good times, he reminded himself, heading the rest of the way up the stairs before she could ask any more questions. His trip down memory lane had started to sink his mood, and he refused to let his father have that kind of power over him. Not ever again.

"Hey, guys," he said, stopping before his old room,

first door on the left, a smile instantly lifting his lips. It looked as though a box factory had exploded.

"Hey, you two," Natalie said, returning his grin somewhat sheepishly as she, too, peered around the room, her hands on her pregnant belly.

"How'd you sleep?" Colt asked with an equally wide smile, getting up from the floor and dodging some boxes. After Colt had finished thumping him on the back, he leaned back and clutched his shoulders. It was good to look into his brother's eyes.

Chance chuckled. "I never made it off the couch."

"You didn't?"

He shook his head. "Just stripped down to my Skivvies and passed out."

He glanced at Carolina. She had the same look on her face as someone who'd just discovered their zipper was down. He almost felt bad for her. Almost. He'd never been one to resist teasing a person.

"Lucky I wasn't naked when Carolina here came bursting through the door this afternoon."

"I didn't burst," she said, tipping her chin up before looking at his brother and his wife. "I thought the place was empty."

"She knew I was half-naked and wanted a glimpse of my hot stud flesh."

Carolina gasped.

"Chance!" his sister-in-law said. "Quit teasing her. You're making her uncomfortable."

He almost said that was the point, but held his tongue. The blush staining Carolina's cheeks was adorable.

Adorable?

Best not to dwell on that too long.

"I'm glad he was able to help you out," Colt said to

Carolina. "Although I think you should start leaving a spare set of keys here."

"I think you're right," she grumbled.

It was then that Chance noticed what his brother and sister-in-law were doing. "Wow."

"Baby equipment," Colt explained, going back to his position on the floor and picking up a screwdriver. "Changing table, crib, a new dresser that should have taken me ten minutes to put together." He rubbed his jaw. "But it's been a little longer than that."

"Because he won't listen." Natalie's blue eyes were clearly teasing.

"Why should I follow the directions?" Colt asked. "Obviously, they're for dummies. We're not dummies. I can figure it out on my own."

Natalie tsked. "Said the man who built the chicken coop that fell down two days later."

Colt shook his head, his eyes seeming to ask the question, *can you believe her?* But he smiled, and Chance had to admit, it was good to see. Colt had waited to join the army until Chance was old enough to get out of the house, too. Claire had already fled, married to Marcus, and so both he and Colt had left for the military together. The difference was that Colt had done only one tour, then returned home to nurse their ailing father—Lord only knew why—while Chance had stayed. Truthfully, the military suited him better. He loved how everything was black-and-white. He relished the camaraderie. The simplicity of being told what to do—and then doing it. His brother hadn't had a good experience in the military, whereas Chance fit in like a foot in a boot. He couldn't wait to go back, this time as a private contractor. More money for doing basically the same job, and a career he loved.

"So what can we do you for?" Colt asked, picking up a small square of wood.

Carolina had been quiet beside him, which struck him as odd. He doubted she was quiet very often, but she seemed to be waiting for him to explain.

"Carolina was wondering if she could sleep in the apartment instead of me."

That stopped Colt. Natalie looked up from reading the directions. They both stared at Carolina with concern.

"Is he back?" Natalie asked.

Carolina nodded, and Chance watched as Carolina's lids caught and held tears. Only she wouldn't let them drop. She straightened her shoulders, clearly getting control of herself. Chance had to admire her for that.

"He left a message on my door," she explained.

That was one way of putting it.

"Well, sure, you can stay anywhere you want," Colt said, glancing at his wife, who nodded. "But where will you sleep?" he asked Chance.

"I was thinking at Claire's place."

"That's too far away," Colt said.

"You can stay here," Natalie interjected. "I mean, if you don't mind pieces of baby equipment and the smell of baby powder and new diapers."

"I told you," Colt said, "I'll have it together in ten minutes."

"That's what you said ten minutes ago."

"I hadn't even started ten minutes ago."

Another long-suffering sigh from Natalie. She caught Chance's eye and smiled.

"I don't mind sleeping in here," Chance said. "I'll

bunk down on the floor, like we used to do when we were kids."

Colt's smile froze. So did Natalie's when she glanced at her husband's face.

They would hide from their dad under the bed, but before that, before their mom died, they'd played games. "You remember the time you couldn't find Henry?"

A smile slipped onto his brother's face. "I do." His gaze encompassed his wife and Carolina. "My pet squirrel. I caught it out back. Stupidest creature that ever walked the earth. Afraid of everything. It must have figured out how to get out of the cage, because one day it was gone."

"We never told Mom," Chance said.

"Nope. Then one day, Chance hears something under his bed."

"Only at night," Chance added. "Thought it was a mouse."

"But it was Henry, and it took us days to catch that damn squirrel again."

That was back before their mom died, back before they'd found her—

Okay, enough. This was part of the reason why he'd come back. He needed to put the ghosts of Christmas past to rest, just as Colt had done.

"We never did tell Mom," Colt said, smiling at Carolina. "She used to get so mad at us for bringing whatever creature we found outside into the house. Remember the lizard?"

Chance grinned. "You mean the one I left in my pocket and that crawled up Mom's arm when she went to do the laundry?"

They both laughed, and Chance caught Natalie staring at them wistfully, a smile on her face, too. "It's good to hear you two reminisce."

"You should have heard our mom shriek," Chance said.

"But she laughed about it," Colt added.

One of the rare times she'd laughed.

"Anyway," Chance said, forcing the memories away. "I already took Carolina home to get some of her things, so I'll just help her settle. Grab my stuff, too. Move in here." Not that he had a whole lot. Just a bag.

"Have at it," Colt said. "But when you're done, I'll expect some help assembling this mess."

"Hey, wait." Natalie frowned. "What is this? *He* can help you, but I'm not allowed?"

Colt scooted toward his wife and rested a hand on her belly. "Because you're pregnant and you should be resting while I do the manly work."

Natalie smiled, the look of love on her face prompting Chance to back out of the room and call out, "Have fun."

He couldn't get out of there fast enough, and he realized he'd forgotten to talk to Natalie about her clients. Oh, well, he'd do it later. Gushy, mushy love always made him uncomfortable. That kind of stuff wasn't for him. He had more important things to do.

"Ready?" he asked Carolina.

She sighed, her pretty blue eyes filling with determination. "As I'll ever be."

Attagirl.

Earlier, when she'd been about to cry, he'd had the damnedest urge to pull her into his arms and hold her tight. He'd wanted to console her and let her know he would protect her.

No chance of that ever happening, he told himself.

No chance at all. He wasn't stupid. Touching Carolina might be a little different than touching other women. He had no idea why that was, but he always listened to his instincts. His instincts told him to keep clear of Carolina Cruthers.

And he planned to heed them.

Chapter Four

It was ridiculously easy to settle into Colt and Natalie's apartment, given that Carolina's tiny two-bedroom apartment had been her home for the past year and a half. Easy, and if she were honest with herself, a relief. No sign of James and no more worries about surprise visits in the middle of the night. Not unless James broke through the iron gate blocking the driveway of Reynolds Ranch and then walked more than two miles to the riding facility. She doubted he'd ever do that, and if he did, they'd see him coming. The only fly in her ointment was her new boss.

Chance Reynolds.

It was as if her thoughts had summoned him.

"Knock, knock?" he called from the other side of her apartment door, adding a rap from his knuckles while she stood in the kitchen, frozen.

Crud.

She was still in her pj's, a gray pair of sweats that hung loose around her waist and had a big hole in the knee. And the T-shirt she wore doubled as a nightie. No bra, either.

"I'll be right there," she called out, making a beeline to the bedroom. Someone had recently decorated the room in a horse motif. She dived beneath a brown-and-black bedspread with a Western star in the middle to find her bra, which she'd apparently ditched atop the bed last night. She felt every second tick as she slipped the thing on, then ran a hand through her loose hair, hoping she looked presentable as she headed to the door.

Presentable? Why? asked a little voice.

She wasn't going to think about that and pasted a smile on her face as she opened the door. "Chance. Hey."

He seemed amused as he eyed her up and down, although what it could be she didn't know. The baggy sweats? Or the messed-up hair? Crud. She hoped her makeup didn't look as if it belonged on *The Walking Dead.* She hadn't even thought about last night's mascara leaving streaks beneath her eyes.

"Took you long enough," he said.

Chance slipped past her, and she ducked back to avoid him touching her.

And there it was.

Attraction. She might as well admit it. Chance Reynolds was more handsome than her boss's good friend Rand Jefferson, a man who played Hawkman in the movies. Whereas Rand had the muscular build of a Greek statue, Chance was more athletic. More Captain America than Hawkman. She much preferred that.

"What's up?" She followed him to the kitchen, where he set down a brown duffel bag, clearly a relic from his past.

"I brought you some presents," he said. "The kind that might save your life."

She caught a glimpse of what was in his bag, something wicked looking and clearly meant for self-defense.

"What kind of weapons do you have in there? I really don't like guns."

"No guns." He held up what looked like an electric razor.

She crossed her arms in front of her. "What am I going to do with that? Shave him to death?"

"Huh?" He glanced at the device in his hand. "Oh. No. It's not a razor." He pressed something on the front. An electronic charge crackled through the air. "It's a Taser."

She straightened in surprise. She'd been thinking about getting one of those.

His smile should be obnoxious this early in the morning. What was it? Seven? But it wasn't obnoxious. It was adorable. He was clearly proud of himself.

"Where did you get it?"

"That's not all I got." He set the Taser down on the table. "There's this, too." He held up a can with a bright red lid. "Pepper spray. There's two kinds. The industrial size." He reached into the bag again. "And the key-chain size. Easier to hold when you're walking alone at night."

Not that she planned on walking anywhere alone. Her curiosity got the better of her, though, and she moved up next to him, fingering the Taser.

"I got it from a friend of mine," Chance said. "Owns a karate studio, but he sells these on the side. Speaking of that, we should teach you some moves. Basic self-defense stuff. You never know when you might need it."

"Brass knuckles?" she said, holding up a feminine version. They'd been painted pink.

He shrugged. "Hey, sometimes simple is best, but I'd have to teach you how to punch in order for them to be effective."

No, thanks. The thought of him touching her in any way, shape or form was…disturbing.

"What's this?" She held up a nasty-looking object with prongs.

"That's the big daddy." His smile was pure, childish delight. "You see these? You can shoot them at your assailant. It's a Taser, too, but it's the kind the police use. Really high voltage. Knock your guy to the ground. The other one is more of a deterrent. It'll hurt like hell, but it won't knock someone to the ground." He took Big Daddy from her. "This one will do some damage."

She didn't know whether to be amused or repulsed by his enthusiasm, although she wished she'd had some of these items before. Some of her amusement faded.

"How about this one?" she asked, spying another small can of something.

"Horn. Blow it if you feel threatened. Usually that's enough to scare away most assailants."

She pursed her lips and moved on. "And this?"

He seemed disappointed. "That's just a flashlight."

Her smile returned. He set Big Daddy on the table, eyeing the smorgasbord of self-defense with a self-satisfied expression.

"What do you think of this?" He held up a key chain in the shape of a cat. "Isn't it cute?"

"Yeah." She studied it. "What does it do? Unfold into a ninja star or something?"

He shook his head. "You hold it like this." He placed the cat in his hand, the points of the ears sliding in between his fingers so that they stuck out from between his knuckles. "Instant shish kebab."

"Nice."

Clearly, it was one of his favorites, at least judging by his small chuckle. "Which one do you like?" he asked.

She followed his gaze, studying the things he'd brought. She should be pleased he hadn't brought her a gun, although she wouldn't be surprised if that weren't in her future, too.

Carolina fingered the big can. "How badly does the pepper spray sting?"

"It's nasty. He'll be blind for hours."

She jerked her hand back. "Blind?"

He dismissed her concerns with a wave. "Unable to open his eyes," he added quickly, "but that's only if you point it at his face. Which you should, but if you don't, it burns the skin, too."

"I see."

"What smells so good?" he asked with a sniff of the air and a mercurial change of subject.

She smiled. "Coffee. Freshly made. Would you like a cup? It's hazelnut flavor."

"Got any food?"

Food? "I, uh. Well, yeah. I have eggs and bacon."

"Perfect. I'll whip us something up while you look things over."

"Wait." *What?* "You don't have to cook."

"I don't mind. I'm used to fending for myself, remember. You should really pick up and handle the items I brought over. Get a feel for them."

And that was how she found herself staring after him in surprise as he opened up her fridge. She huffed in resignation.

While Chance cooked breakfast, Carolina touched each self-defense mechanism. She sighed quietly. Maybe it was *his* kitchen. He was the one that should have been living in the apartment. But as she picked up each of the items, she remembered how Colt's sister had told her about the time her fiancé had made her breakfast while her son was really sick. They hadn't been together back then. It'd just been a kind gesture. Carolina remembered thinking she'd never find a man to do something so nice. Despite women's so-called liberation, the men she'd been dating reverted right back to the Stone Age. Women did the cooking, cleaning and laundry. And yet here she was, watching the most gorgeous male she'd ever seen flip eggs in a pan like some kind of master chef.

She wanted to kiss him.

Not because she hoped to start something, but because she was so very thankful for his concern. She might have been annoyed and humiliated yesterday to learn her boss wanted him to be her bodyguard, but she'd thank Colt later when she saw him. The worry and fear that James would come back were gone. And now she would have some form of protection. All in all, things were looking up—thanks to Chance.

"So, what did you decide?" he asked, setting down a plate of heavenly smelling eggs and bacon in front of her. "Which one do you want?"

"Well, it's a toss-up between Hello Kitty the weapon and the pepper spray."

"Take both."

She didn't know why she felt self-conscious as she touched the cat-shaped weapon, but she did. She set it down, unable to resist digging into her breakfast. But as she lifted her fork, she suddenly took great care not to get any on her lips because for some reason she felt terribly exposed.

"I can't afford both, I'm sure," she said, making sure she didn't chew with her mouth open or something.

"You don't have to pay for them. They're gifts. From me."

"I can't accept them."

He was busy gobbling down his own breakfast. "Sure you can," he said between swallows. "I get all this stuff at cost. Part of my new job. I'll be outfitting my clients with these types of weapons."

She lifted the bacon to her lips, spotted him watching her again, and her cheeks heated up. Why was he staring at her? She took a bite and then set the bacon down, even though she just about groaned at how good it tasted. Golly, the man could heat up a room with the look in his eyes.

"Still," she said. "I don't want to take advantage. Even at cost, I doubt I could afford any of it."

He didn't say anything, and when she finally got the nerve to look up at him, she noticed the most bizarre expression on his face.

"What?" she asked.

He rubbed his chin. "Ah. Yeah. Like I said. I'll take care of it. You can pay me back slowly if you want."

"Chance—"

"No arguments," he interrupted. "This is your safety we're talking about. You need to be prepared."

She couldn't argue that point, so she continued eating her breakfast, feeling his gaze upon her all over again. Man, she wished he'd stop watching her.

"Thank you," she said once she finished.

"You're welcome," he said, shooting up suddenly with his plate in hand.

"I'll wash that."

"No. That's okay. I've got it. Here. Give me yours."

She handed him the empty plate. He hurried to the sink and, sure enough, washed her dishes for her. As she sat in her chair, she stared at the weapons and wondered why she'd never been able to find a man like Chance. Just her luck he was leaving for the Middle East in a short while. And that he was her boss's brother. And that he knew about James and so probably had a low opinion of her life choices. So if that was a spark of attraction in his eyes, she knew he'd never act on it.

"Thanks," she said, standing.

He grabbed a rag and dried his hands, but when he met her gaze, he seemed to freeze.

"I mean it, Chance. You've really taken a load off my mind. I'd been thinking about getting some pepper spray. Now I don't have to worry. And if I get in a bind, I have Ninja Kitty to poke James's eyes out with."

He didn't say anything, but then seemed to nudge himself back to life, tossing the towel he held to the counter. "Protecting people is my job."

Something about the way he said the words made her tilt her head. He seemed upset, as if he were disappointed in something…maybe her?

"I should get going," he said, moving past her.

"Chance, wait."

It was one of those moments when you call someone back and you don't know why. When you know you want to say something, but you don't know what. When words form, only to be immediately discarded. She'd already thanked him.

"I'll ask Colt to take what I owe you out of my next paycheck."

He nodded. "Whatever." He slipped out the door.

What had she done? Something had definitely soured his mood. He couldn't get away from her fast enough. Only after he left did she realize he'd left all his weapons behind.

Chapter Five

Three days later she was no closer to solving the riddle of Chance. They were slated to work together, and she was a little nervous. She watched him from a distance as he and Colt gave direction from the side of his trailer, which was parked in the middle of the arena. Colt had just taught Chance the part of the skit where Teddy stole the handkerchief out of Chance's back pocket. Usually, the next part of the act was Teddy jumping in the trailer by himself. Only the horse had refused to load.

"I swear he's like a petulant kid," she heard Colt say as he gave the signal for Teddy to load up for the fourth time. A signal that was ignored. Teddy stood, handkerchief in his mouth, and any time one of the men approached him, he ran away. This, too, was part of the act, and when Colt told the horse to stop and to come to him—the last part of their act together—Teddy usually obeyed. Not today.

"He gets in these moods," Colt said. "But he always performs when it's for real. I've never had him duck out on me or nothin'. I swear he likes the applause."

They were out of doors on a day so calm and clear it looked like a masterfully painted backdrop of a movie set: bright blue sky, puffy clouds that dotted the ground with their shadows, mountains in the distance. Carolina had once visited her friend Sam on location. They'd been filming a scene with her husband against a fake background so similar it felt eerie. The only difference today was they were surrounded by a carpet of green, not asphalt, and the emerald-colored grass was thanks to the irrigation system that was the envy of their neighbors—and made the ranch worth a small fortune. Colt had been offered a sweet deal to sell the place but had flatly refused. It was a family homestead, and he planned to keep it that way, or so she'd been told by Sam.

"He's a character, all right," Chance said.

"Teddy, knock it off."

Carolina could hear the exasperation in Colt's voice. Apparently, Teddy could, too, because he dropped the handkerchief and trotted over to Colt as if that had been his plan all along. "You nut," Colt said, but he patted the horse's neck and smiled.

Chance crossed his arms. "Okay, so normally the act ends with Teddy jumping in the trailer while the Galloping Girlz enter the arena, but you want to change all that, so what does it matter if he loads up or not?"

Colt nodded. "You're right. It doesn't matter. I'm looking forward to jazzing up the routine. People have seen the old act a million times."

Chance tipped his cowboy hat back, hands on his hips. It didn't seem fair that a man who'd been off the ranch for almost a decade could look so good in a cowboy hat and jeans. But Chance did. Carolina wondered if the boots he wore had been his before he'd joined the army.

"You'll get the hang of it. And Teddy will behave when you're out on the road."

"I'm sure I will."

Colt waved for Carolina to come closer. "You ready to learn the new part?"

"As ready as I'll ever be," she said because she really didn't want to work with Chance. After their breakfast together, things had changed. Sure, it was one-sided. She doubted he felt anything other than mild annoyance that he had to babysit her. But she had developed a full-blown crush. And they'd be working side by side—for hours.

Carolina slipped between the rails of the wooden fence, glancing at the covered arena on the other side of the barn. Lessons were in full swing. Carolina heard Natalie calling to one of her clients as she schooled her horse over a jump. Something about weight in the heels and keeping her hips open—whatever that meant. The smell of dust and a water-soaked pasture filled the air.

"All right," Colt said. "Chance, you're up first. I need you to try and swing up on old Teddy here without a saddle."

Chance eyed the animal skeptically. "He doesn't have a bridle on."

"I'm aware of that, Chance," Colt said, deadpan. "Perhaps that's why I want you to climb aboard, so you can practice riding him without a bridle."

The skin between his brows wrinkled. "Won't he run off?"

"Just do as I ask, please."

Chance studied the horse as if contemplating the odds of his brother's request being a prank. Satisfied with what he saw, he moved forward. "You know, the last time you told me to do as you asked, you blew the toilet seat off with me on it."

Colt chuckled. "This is different."

Chance grabbed a hank of mane. He shifted around a bit, as if trying to recall the position he needed to be in to complete his task. With a deep breath and a giant heave, he threw his leg over the horse, slipped, and almost fell to his knees. He shot them both a grimace before trying again. To Carolina's complete shock, he swung up the next time as if he'd been doing it his whole life, and maybe he had.

"Wow," his brother said. "Impressive."

All week long, Carolina had told herself there was no way Colt's idea for a new routine would work, not when his brother hadn't ridden in years. And yet there Chance sat, staring down at her triumphantly, looking as if he belonged on an old Western movie poster with his black hat and denim shirt. All he'd need was a black eye mask to be a Western hero like the Lone Ranger.

"Okay, that was easy," Chance said. "What's next?"

"Bill the Barrel Man. He's going to play the part of bad guy."

"Yeah, but he's not here."

"You'll have to use your imagination."

"I didn't know that man was still around," Chance said.

"Still going strong after all these years. We follow the same rodeo schedule, which is why this'll work out great. He actually seemed a little excited about joining in on our routine. Said we can practice it when we're at the rodeo this next weekend." Colt turned toward the middle of the arena and pointed. "Bill's going to be off on the sidelines dressed as Dastardly Dan."

"Who?"

Colt waved away his brother's question. "You'll be just finishing up your act with Teddy. The Galloping

Girlz will be announced. Carolina will ride in as if all is well. She'll stand up on Rio's back, only Bill will jump out of his barrel and grab her horse's bridle or something. We'll have to work out the details of that. I want it to look kind of like Pitiful Pearl."

"Pitiful Pearl?" Chance asked.

His brother released a long-suffering sigh of impatience. "You know, like those old black-and-white movies without the sound. Overacted skit. Lots of arm waving and facial expressions. Caro will be perfect."

"Caro?" Chance asked, eyeing her anew.

She had a hard time meeting his gaze. "It's what my friends call me."

He smiled wickedly. "I could be your friend."

Oh, dear Lord in heaven.

He was teasing, she knew that, just as she knew his words shouldn't affect her, not after everything she'd been through. Yet they did. The man was too gorgeous for his own good.

"Anyway," Colt said, eyeing the two of them askance. "Caro will be pulled from her horse…somehow. I want you to swing up on Teddy and rescue her."

"Rescue her how?"

"You know, ride up to her at breakneck speed, clasp her hand, then swing her up behind you. Like in the movies. Then you'll ride back to the trailer and Caro will grab a rope. She'll stand up on the back of Teddy and the two of you will set off, and she'll rope Bill and drag him back to his barrel, or maybe out of the arena. I haven't decided yet. And not really drag. He can sort of be walking, but pretending to fight you the whole time. We'll have to see what looks best." He turned toward his brother. "My biggest concern is your riding skills.

We'll need to work on them. It might take a while before you're in the proper shape to lift Caro up from a run."

"Nah. I'm in the best shape of my life." He patted his abs.

Carolina realized she chewed on the end of her hair again and flicked the strands away, thinking Chance was right. She remembered what he'd looked like without his shirt on, and it still gave her hot flashes.

Colt didn't seem as convinced. "I don't doubt for a minute you can run a mile, but riding a horse is different."

"Oh, yeah?"

"Don't get your knickers in a twist—"

Chance dug his heels in Teddy's sides. It was like a scene straight out of an old Western. Teddy shot off, though quite frankly, the horse probably bolted more out of shock than anything else. The biggest surprise was how well Chance rode. Well, for about five seconds. Teddy turned right. Quickly. Chance listed to the left.

"Oh, no!"

He landed with an *oomph*.

Colt's laughter filled the air. Carolina almost ran toward Chance, but Colt stopped her, the sideways look he shot her full of amusement. "This is going to be fun."

IF HE LANDED on his butt one more time, he would shoot himself. God bless it. And in front of Caro, too.

Caro. He liked the nickname. Just as he enjoyed watching her eat bacon.

Ump. Stop it.

He'd told himself he would keep his mind out of the gutter today. Had convinced himself it was just his long hitch in the army that had him practically combusting on the spot when he'd watched her slide that damn piece of pork in her mouth.

"Just let go of the mane," his brother ordered.

Focus. You'll fall on your ass again if you keep thinking about Caro's mouth.

"You'll never get better if you use your hands to hang on and not your legs."

Chance released an oath of frustration, although if he were honest, it wasn't simply because of his trouble riding. "I told you. I can't hold on unless I'm grabbing the mane."

They'd been at it for over an hour, and Chance had lost count of how many times he'd fallen off. Everything was fine at a walk and a trot. There was just something about Teddy's lope that threw him off balance, especially in the corners.

"Maybe we should work through things at a walk," Carolina suggested, looking like a pink candy cane in her curve-hugging spandex suit, which reminded Chance there was other things she could stick in her mouth.

STOP!

He needed to get control of his wayward thoughts.

"Yeah, you're right," his brother said. "At this rate, you and I will be old and gray before he learns how to ride again."

"I know how to ride."

His brother turned to Carolina, so Chance couldn't see his face, but he must have made a derogatory expression, because Carolina bit her lip, then looked at the ground—as if she didn't want him to see the amusement in her eyes.

"Fine."

Okay, so yeah, it was humiliating to keep falling off

in front of the oh-so-gorgeous Caro, but at least he got back up and tried it again.

Colt turned back around to face him. "Let's do a run-through of the act."

Carolina still wouldn't look up at him, not even when he rode up next to her and Colt.

Colt patted Teddy's neck. "Let's take it from the part where Caro swings up behind you."

"Good. Fine. Whatever." What did it matter if she was privately laughing at him? It wasn't as if he was trying to impress her or anything.

His brother turned toward Carolina. "When you get on, stand up. Chance will do a big circle around me. If you're feeling brave, Chance, try it at a trot. Maybe Caro can help keep you balanced."

Chance held out his hand. Carolina played peeka-boo with her eyes, glancing at him once, then twice, but never holding his gaze. She slapped her palm into his, and as Chance wrapped his fingers around hers and pulled her toward him, he experienced the strangest sensation. He froze for a moment—something that seemed to keep happening around her—and it made him wonder if the jet lag had affected him worse than he'd thought.

Or maybe he'd simply bumped his head one too many times during today's rehearsal.

"Ready?" he asked Caro.

She nodded. He pulled, and with an ease that left him in awe, she slid on behind him. Seriously. It was as if she had a magnet on her butt. The feel of her warm body up against his own, the suit she wore so thin it was like having her naked…

STOP.

He needed to take a deep breath. Big mistake. She smelled like Downy fabric softener. He'd always loved the smell of that stuff.

"Are you okay?" she asked.

"Fine."

One. Two. Three.

He did the same thing when he was out on the gun range. Counted down to calm his mind and get his brain focused.

"You're just really good," he added. Good to feel up against him, he privately added.

"She's a professional," Colt said, staring up at them both. "Caro, go ahead and stand."

Chance felt hands on his shoulders. There was a moment when he caught a whiff of her perfume or body cream or whatever it was she wore, and it blended with the smell of her hair. It had been a long, long time since he'd smelled something that smelled like, well, a woman.

Honeysuckle.

That was it. The kind that used to grow alongside what was now the hay barn. His mom had loved that honeysuckle. Chance had loved it, too. His dad had ripped it down in a fit of anger.

"Okay, good," Colt said. "Chance, go ahead and walk."

He was so deep in his thought, it took him a moment to hear Colt's words. Caro was all business, already standing up behind him.

"Let's trot instead." Chance dug his heels into Teddy's side.

"No," Caro said. "Wait. Maybe we should—"

Whatever she'd been about to say was cut off by

the fact that he'd started to slip off to the side again. He pulled himself toward the middle. Carolina clearly thought he was in trouble, though, because her hands gripped his denim shirt, as if she planned to physically hold him in place.

"I'm all right," he told her.

She let go. He somehow managed to stay put, because he'd be damned if he fell off while she stood up— actually stood up on two feet—behind him. Talk about humiliation. He wondered if she knew how often he got up in the middle of the night to check on her, just in case that crazy ex of hers showed up. He might suck at riding, but nobody better mess around with him when it came to protecting what was his. Well, not *his*, but his responsibility. That's for sure.

"That's good," Colt said. "Caro, quit worrying about him. He's not going to fall off. Chance, use your body weight to guide Teddy toward me. See if Caro can grab the rope."

Rope? What rope? Somewhere in the middle of all this Colt had snatched a rope from the horse trailer. He held it out. Chance shifted his weight to the left, relieved when Teddy obeyed the silent instructions and headed for his owner. Chance's legs were growing weak, and though he hated to do it, he grabbed Teddy's mane. Maybe the horse sensed Chance's growing desperation to prove himself in front of Carolina, or maybe he was hanging on so hard Teddy became confused, but one minute they were trotting and the next Teddy was in a lope.

"Whoa, whoa, whoa," he told the horse, pulling back on the animal's mane as if it were the reins.

"Lean back," Colt yelled.

He couldn't lean back. Carolina was there. "Teddy, whoa!" he heard her order.

But it was no use. Worse, he could feel himself slipping. Carolina clutched the fabric at his shoulders, and damned if she didn't hold him in place for a stride or two, but he was too much deadweight.

"Caro, let go!" Colt shouted.

The stubborn woman refused to listen, and Chance knew they were both going down.

"Shit."

It was the last word he said before he fell. Caro said something, too, but he didn't catch it because he hit the ground hard, and he'd somehow managed to land on his back, and then, in that strange way that time seemed to slow down when something bad happened, he saw Carolina fall toward him. He reached for her, used his arms to absorb the impact, but she still landed on top of him with an *oomph*.

They both lay there, trying to catch their breath. She lifted her head, and the world did that freezing, dizzy thing. She peered into his eyes, inches away, and it didn't matter she had a crazy ex-boyfriend and Chance had no intention of sticking around. Nothing mattered except the color of her eyes, the way the sunlight touched her skin, turning it as translucent as a pearl. Nothing mattered except how her body felt in that skintight costume and the way his body responded.

"Sorry." He abruptly thrust her away.

"You guys okay?" Colt asked, running up to them.

"I'm done," Chance said, hopping to his feet. He held out a hand for Caro. He didn't want to, but he did it anyway. She took it, and he actually felt relief.

Relief!

It was in that instant Chance realized he might have a problem. A big problem—and her name was Carolina Cruthers.

Chapter Six

Clearly, the man didn't like her, or maybe he was just embarrassed by his lackluster performance. Carolina didn't know, but a week later, as they set to depart for a rodeo, she realized she missed the Chance who had teased her in the kitchen.

"You ready?" he asked, slamming the door of Colt's truck. She glanced back at the Rodeo Misfits trailer hooked up behind them. The competition didn't start until tomorrow. She and Chance were to go ahead and set up camp and settle the horses. The other girls would make their own way north later in the afternoon.

Colt's plan was to perform with Carolina this weekend, then for Chance to take over next weekend, but she feared that wouldn't happen. Every time they'd practiced, Chance had fallen off. Not as much as he had that first day, since he'd been practicing with his old rope horse, Frosty, to get himself in better shape. But he wasn't quite ready. If Chance fell off just once during the performance, it would ruin the act. Her boss knew it. Chance knew it, too, and Carolina wondered if that was what had soured his mood.

"Let's hit it," she said with a smile.

He didn't respond, and she tried not to feel offended

again. No matter what bothered the man, she still owed him a huge debt of gratitude. She hadn't seen James in over a week, and she felt reassured by the can of pepper spray in her purse and the Hello Kitty on her key chain. He hadn't been by the ranch, either, and she'd taken matters into her own hands and changed her cell phone number, which had stopped the texts. With any luck, he'd given up on his scare tactics, too. She could go back to her own place on Monday and quit having to depend on others for help.

Quit having to be around Chance. Well, except on weekends. And during their practice sessions. And when they traveled to rodeos together.

Okay, maybe she wouldn't be able to avoid him.

"Listen," she said as they pulled out of the driveway, light dots of water sprinkling the windshield. Coastal fog—common in the fall—had pushed its misty fingers inland and covered the land like a kid hiding his eyes. It would be like this every morning until spring came along. "I don't think I ever really said thank you."

He glanced at her quickly. She kept her gaze off him, too. They were leaving Misfit Farms behind them, the white fences on both sides of the road a muted gray.

She sighed. "I'm sure this wasn't how you hoped to spend your time Stateside, babysitting me."

He shook his head. "I'll tell you how I didn't plan to spend my time." His expression was wry as he glanced at her again. "Falling on my ass every five minutes."

Was that what bothered him? Wounded male pride?

"It's not every five minutes," she said, smiling again. "It's every ten."

His expression said it all. *Great. Thanks.*

"But you're doing good considering it's been nearly ten years since you've ridden."

"It's not the riding that's the problem," he said. "It's when you climb onboard that I get into trouble."

It was true. He'd been able to lope Teddy around on his own for the past two days, but when she jumped up behind him, it threw him off.

"You'll figure it out."

"Better be soon. Colt doesn't want to have to leave the ranch again, what with Wes and Jillian's upcoming wedding and Natalie about to pop. Colt's the best man and has too much to do. They should have done a shotgun wedding in someone's backyard like Colt and Natalie did." Carolina had heard about the infamous wedding. They'd surprised everyone after a charity event held at the ranch. They'd been married in front of every A-list celebrity in Hollywood, many of whom still popped by, including Rand Jefferson. But that was to be expected, Caro reminded herself. Rand had married her friend Sam, one of the former Galloping Girlz, and Sam couldn't resist coming out and riding with the girls from time to time. Carolina had gotten used to having a world-famous actor as a friend.

"How long have you known Wes and Jillian?" she asked.

It was because of Jillian that Natalie had met Colt. From what she'd heard, Colt had been happy living a life secluded on the ranch, his sister less than a mile away, and only leaving on the weekends to perform. Natalie had been in a bad horse accident, and Wes and Jillian had suggested Colt could help her learn to ride again. They'd fallen in love along the way. And the rest was history.

"I've known Wes my whole life," Chance said. "His

mom was friends with our mom, but he's mostly my brother's friend."

"Wes seems nice," Carolina observed. "And Jillian is amazing with animals. Once one of Natalie's jumping horses was limping and they couldn't figure out why. Jillian came over and told her it was a torn muscle. They took the horse to the vet clinic, and Mariah used some kind of infrared device to confirm the diagnosis. It was unreal."

"I've heard it's crazy how good Jillian is reading animals."

It was the first conversation—their first real conversation—since their practice session in the arena. She smiled. She liked talking to him. It was easy. Not awkward and uncomfortable. "I think she does more than simply read them. It's almost like she can talk to them or something."

"Dr. Doolittle," Chance said. "That's what Colt calls her."

"Exactly like—"

She bolted upright in her seat. Chance slowed down as quickly as he could with horses in the back of the trailer. They'd reached the end of the drive and the iron gates that guarded the entrance of Reynolds Ranch. In the distance was James's truck.

Son of a—

Chance must have realized who it was, too, as she'd given him a detailed description of James's truck, as well as a picture of the man himself. It might still be early enough that the headlights painted the pavement gray, but James's big silver truck was hard to miss. Her ex must have realized they'd spotted him, because suddenly his lights flicked on. He peeled out so fast his tires kicked up a stream of dust and rubber.

"Damn," Chance said.

Yes, damn. She'd truly hoped he'd leave her alone now. That he'd had his fun. But being faced with the reality of James's presence was like discovering a gaping hole in her arm, one so big and ghastly she didn't know how it could ever be fixed.

"I don't understand," she whispered.

They both watched as James sped off, his taillights fading to small points of light before disappearing altogether.

She clenched her fists. "Why won't he leave me alone?"

The side of Chance's jaw ticked, his eyes slits as he stared at the spot where James had been parked.

"Bastard's gonna be sorry."

SHE HARDLY SAID a word the rest of the ride. That was okay. Chance was busy checking his six, even doubling back once, not that she seemed to notice. Carolina seemed too lost in her own thoughts, fiddling with a strand of her hair, probably wondering what she could do to keep James away.

Nothing.

The simple truth was, there were some men who didn't want to take no for an answer. Who were crazy. Who did things no sane man would ever do. Over there, in the Middle East, Chance had seen things. He shook his head, not wanting to think about it. Suffice to say, he'd probably taken James a hell of a lot more seriously than she had, knowing what he knew about certain individuals.

He gripped the steering wheel. "I won't let him hurt you."

"He knows where the rodeo is," she said in a small voice.

He glanced at her, about to ask how that was possible, when he realized she was right. Of course he knew. Colt's rodeo schedule was posted online. It was no big secret where they would be. And even if it hadn't been online, rodeos had their own websites, and they listed who their performers would be. He was an idiot for not thinking of that sooner. Of course, he'd been hoping the guy had given up. The sight of him sitting in front of the gate had changed all that. It'd been nearly two weeks since Carolina had moved to the ranch, and James clearly still had it out for her. That meant he was capable of anything. Maybe even scary things. Like the stuff Chance had seen while serving.

"If he shows up, I'll take care of him."

She nodded, her gaze firmly fixed ahead.

"In the meantime, maybe you should call the lieutenant in charge of your case."

"I will once we get there."

"Not that it'll do any good," he said, checking his six once again as he merged onto a new road. "James's gonna do whatever he wants. His type of man always does. He's mad at you for breaking up with him, and he's trying to make you pay."

She stared out the front windshield, clearly oblivious to what was around her. "I never should have started seeing him."

"Hindsight is always twenty-twenty."

"Yeah, but I wasn't even looking to get involved with someone. From day one, my whole focus has been the

Galloping Girlz. When he asked me out on a date, I actually said no."

"Sometimes you can have a gut feeling about someone."

They were headed into the Sierra foothills, to a town whose claim to fame was the rodeo they held every fall. It was getting to the end of rodeo season. Any cowboy that found himself behind in earnings would be at the Tres Rios grounds in the hopes of a last-minute score of cash that might nudge them toward the top of the standings, and the National Finals Rodeo.

Carolina hugged herself. "When we first started dating, he was really charming."

Chance simply nodded, keeping quiet. He sensed she wanted to talk to someone. He would listen.

"We had so much fun. He was so attentive, and I liked that. I'd never met a man who so clearly wanted to spend time with me, but then it got to be a little annoying. One day, I decided to go out to a bar with everyone in our group. I wasn't planning on picking up anybody or dancing. It was just a night of fun for us girls to relax, you know, away from a rodeo or practicing out at Colt's place."

She shook her head, her lips pressing together for a moment. Her hands clenched.

"James told me I couldn't go." She looked at him then. "I laughed."

She shook her head again, her gaze shifting to the scenery in front of them once more—the mountains in the distance capped with snow, the hills nearest them scorched brown by the California sun—her face as cold as the stone in the hillside.

"He hit me. *Bam.*" She mimicked the motion of being

struck in the head. "One minute, I was standing, and the next, I was on the ground. I remember thinking, *did he really just do that?* Only he had, and then he was holding me and telling me how sorry he was, and I wanted to believe him..."

So she'd forgiven him. She didn't need to say the words. Chance knew she'd let him back into her life, as many women did with their partners.

"He was good to me after that, and I started to think he'd just had a bad day. You know, that I must have pushed him too hard. That it was somehow my fault." She pinned him with a stare, her gaze so intense it was as if she tried to turn back time with her mind. "It's amazing how easy it was to believe it was a onetime thing. Two months later, he hit me again, and that was the time I told him to go to hell, only he didn't take the news well."

She touched the side of her face this time, as if touching invisible scars. "Thank God one of my neighbors came along when he did. He said he'd heard my screams. I honestly don't know if James would have stopped. I ended up in the hospital. I don't remember much about how I got there. The police came. I filed charges. I thought James would leave me alone after that, especially since he'd be in jail, but the bastard posted bail the next day and then he was out and the phone calls started."

"He's angry."

"I'm the one who should be angry." She inhaled, a sigh of resignation and possibly disgust. "But I'm scared."

"Don't be." He'd said the word so sharply she had immediately turned to look at him. "Don't be afraid. I haven't served eight years protecting this country to let some lowlife scumbag push you around. He has no idea who he's messing with."

He was driving, which made it hard to maintain eye contact, but he did his best, and he hoped she saw how serious he was.

Carolina swiped at her eyes. "He's going to make an appearance at the rodeo. How much do you want to bet?"

"I'm not going to take that bet. Not when I think you're right."

She pulled her legs up onto the bench seat and hugged her knees. "Maybe I shouldn't perform."

"Don't," he said again, just as sharply. "You've changed your life around enough already. Don't let him take this away from you, too."

He didn't realize what he was doing until he did it. He pulled over to the side of the two-lane county road.

"What's the matter?" she asked.

"First of all," he said, stopping the truck, "I'm checking to make sure he's not following us. With the hill behind us the way it is, he'll crest the top before he realizes we've pulled over."

She glanced behind them, trying to see through the horse trailer and the road beyond. "I noticed you doubled back earlier, but he's not following, is he?"

"Not yet. But he might have been smart. Might have left ahead of us, but I think you're right. He knows exactly where we're going. Sitting outside the gate this morning was his way of telling you he knows your schedule, and man, I'd like to beat his face into a pulp because of it."

She looked ahead again, still hugging her knees.

"But I won't, because there's more than one way to skin a cat."

He rested a hand on her knee, and she jumped. He hated that she jumped. This week, he'd done his best to keep his distance from her. Easier to do that, considering his inconvenient attraction to her. However, trying to maintain space hadn't helped his concentration riding Teddy. He'd fallen off more times than a drunk on a bar stool. Still, his need to comfort Carolina in that moment outweighed his common sense, and he squeezed her leg. She looked up at him, and those blue, blue eyes drew him down and down and down, and it wasn't until he was inches away from her face that he realized he'd dropped his head toward her own. And that she hadn't moved away while he did so.

He shot back so fast he nearly clocked his head on the driver-side window.

"Sorry." If he hadn't been wearing a cowboy hat, he would have run his fingers through his hair. "I was just going to say everything will be okay."

She nodded in agitation, and it was then that Chance got his second shock where Carolina Cruthers was concerned.

She was attracted to him, too.

Chapter Seven

He'd almost kissed her.

Carolina was certain of it.

Thank God he'd stopped himself. But *why* had he stopped? It was driving her nuts. It shouldn't. She should be grateful. It was too soon. Way too soon to be thinking about kissing another guy. What was she? Crazy? And he was leaving in a couple of months. She couldn't have picked a worse possible man to have a crush on.

But crush on him she did, and she was beginning to think he might have noticed.

He had hardly said two words since he'd started the truck and pulled back onto the highway. Had he seen her cheeks fill with color? Had he noticed the way her breathing had quickened? Did he know she'd become frozen with anticipation as his head had lowered toward her own? It wasn't right. They'd been talking about her twisted ex-boyfriend, for goodness' sake. She should have sworn off men for the rest of her life, not been practically panting the first time someone new tried to kiss her.

"I'll unload the horses." He put the truck in Park again, this time out back behind the rodeo grounds.

"I'll check in with the rodeo manager. Find out where it's okay to set up."

He nodded. She waited for him to look her in the eyes, and when he didn't, tried not to let her disappointment show as she inhaled a deep breath of pine-scented air. What a messed-up piece of work she'd turned out to be.

But he doesn't know about that other thing.

And he wouldn't, either. She would make sure of it, she vowed, heading for the rodeo office.

"Well, lookee here," said Hank Havens, a person who characterized the epitome of a rodeo man. Big hat, wide girth, cheesy smile. "If it isn't Spider Woman in the flesh."

Spider Woman. The nickname he'd given her when she'd nearly had a wreck with her horse, somehow managing to hang on to the underside of her horse's neck during the middle of a performance. That was when she'd first started out with the Galloping Girlz. She thanked the Lord it hadn't ended badly.

"Hey, Hank." She forced a smile. "Just checking in."

The man had the eyes of a laser scanner, and they beamed up and down, the wrinkles beneath his oversize cowboy hat deepening. "Why, you look as miserable as a herd of wet cattle."

She tried to muster a smile. She truly did. "Been a long drive."

His gray eyes narrowed, and she knew he didn't believe her. She toyed with telling him all about James, but she hated to drag him into the whole mess. She didn't want anyone to know how stupid she'd been.

"Okay if we toss the horses in one of the stock contractor pens?" she asked.

Hank's big jowls quivered for a moment, as if he were

about to say something. Then he smiled. "Why, sure. 'Course, honey. You don't even have to ask."

She slipped outside before he could probe deeper and took a calming breath when she paused outside the portable trailer that served as the rodeo office. They were only an hour off the main highway, but it felt as if they were hours away from anywhere.

The rodeo grounds were in a clearing ringed by tall pine trees. A massive arena was in the middle of it all. Grandstands stair-stepped their way toward the sky. It seemed like such an arbitrary location, as if God had plopped down a tiny toy rodeo play set in the middle of nowhere. Truth was, they were surrounded by a small logging town. There were homes in the hills around them, and one of the nation's biggest sawmills was not far away. The townspeople loved their rodeo, too. They would celebrate tonight by hosting a big rodeo dance, an event Carolina always avoided like the plague.

James stood in front of her.

She almost screamed, realizing too late that it was actually Chance.

"Did I scare you?"

He knew he had, but she still said, "No."

He'd removed his hat. A red ring from the hat indented his forehead. He'd fluffed up his hair, too, and she realized he'd tried to look like her ex on purpose.

"Where's your cat key chain?"

"In my purse. In the truck."

"Good place for it."

"I was just walking to the rodeo office."

"You could be walking to an outhouse and be attacked, which is why you need to carry it around with you at all times," he said sternly. "Don't go around with your head down. Look up and survey your surroundings, and most of all, be prepared."

He was still angry, although not at her, she realized. At James. Something about that anger stirred feelings in her own heart.

"I'm sorry."

"Don't apologize." He tipped her chin up with his hand. Her breath caught. "This is *not* your fault. None of this is the result of something *you* did. He's a lowlife piece of scum, and if he comes near you, he'll be sorry."

How was it possible to be so afraid of one man and yet so incredibly attracted to another at the same time?

Crazy.

"He won't come here." The words were more of an affirmation, one she'd been repeating to herself the whole way there.

"If he does, I'll take care of it."

Chance never looked away, and she took this time to examine his face. He looked more like his sister, Claire, than his brother, with his green eyes and dark hair. But it was the expression on his face that held her attention. She'd never seen such a look of fierce determination—and it was all aimed at protecting her.

Frankly, it turned her on.

SLEEPING ARRANGEMENTS.

He'd been thinking about it the whole damn way to the rodeo. It hadn't been a problem before he'd damn near kissed her. But now he'd be a fool to share a room with her, not when he clearly couldn't be trusted to keep his distance. No. It'd be better if he found her a hotel room or another place to stay, or a place for him to stay. There was just one problem.

James.

What if he showed up in the middle of the night? What if he watched her bunk down in someone else's trailer? What if he sneaked up on her? Chance couldn't allow that to happen, which meant sticking to Carolina like glue, which meant sharing the trailer with her.

Yippee-ki-yay!

So when she showed up at the trailer after a quick practice session with the girls, he needed to tell her his plan. She wore that skintight bodysuit he was growing to hate, or maybe love, and he tried not to notice the way it showed off her every curve. "Look, I was thinking you might be uncomfortable with me sleeping inside. You know, gossip and all that, so I was going to grab a blanket and set up camp outside."

"What?" She appeared genuinely surprised, the evening sun shining into her blue eyes. "I don't care what people think."

"Well, I do. I'll keep watch out here."

"Not going to happen." She crossed her arms over her chest, apparently digging in her heels over the issue. "People can gossip all they want. I already owe you so much. I'm not going to be responsible for booting you from your bed."

He didn't like the images the word *bed* provoked. "I thought with everything that had happened between you and James, you might be uncomfortable sleeping with a strange man. I mean, sleeping near a man you don't know all that well."

Why did he feel like a bumbling fool all of a sudden? Was it the fact she stood, blue eyes wide, blond hair streaming down her back, her body silhouetted by the sun?

"You're my boss's brother." She forced a smile. He could tell by the way it didn't quite wrinkle the corners of her eyes. "It'll be fine."

Somehow he doubted that.

"I promise not to bite," she added.

Yeah, but would he be able to keep from biting her? That was the question.

SHE'D BEEN LYING. It would not be fine. She recognized that fact within two minutes of stepping inside the trailer.

"I need to take a shower," she announced.

He'd followed her inside, but her words made him freeze. "Oh, yeah. Sure. I'll wait outside while you do that."

For a fraction of a second, she wondered what he would do if she invited him into the shower with her, but as quickly as the thought came, she chased it away. She did not need that type of complication in her life, not matter how tempting.

"Thanks," she said instead, forcing another smile.

The moment he closed the trailer door, she leaned her head against a nearby cabinet and groaned. This weekend was not going how she'd planned. She'd meant to keep her cool, to treat him like a big brother, to shove her damn physical attraction to the furthest reaches of her mind, where she'd slap a giant iron bolt across it and never think about it again.

Ha.

Carolina took a cold shower. When she finished, she pulled clothes out of her duffel bag. She layered on item after item, partly because she was freezing and partly because it would act as barricade against her own desires. She hoped.

"Your turn," she said, stepping outside, hair still wet from the shower. She shivered in the cool night air. "I'll wait out here while you do your thing."

Chance frowned. He obviously didn't like the idea of leaving her alone.

"And look," she said, holding up her Hello Kitty key chain. "I brought protection." She patted the pocket of her sweats. Well, the first layer of sweats. "And pepper spray. I promise to scream if James makes an appearance."

"Just the same, I would feel better if you were inside with me."

While he took a shower? No, thanks. That was all she needed, to imagine water sluicing over his arms and belly and…other things. While she wondered what it would be like to glide her fingers down—

She swallowed. "I'll wait here."

He must have realized she wasn't going to heed his wishes, because he glanced around them once—as if searching the bushes for James—before turning toward the trailer.

"Stay by the door," he ordered.

"Yes, sir!" She saluted.

"I'll be quick." She waited a full minute before patting her other pocket and then pulling her cell phone out. With a deep breath and a silent prayer, she dialed the familiar number, grateful her number was blocked from caller ID. James answered after the second ring.

"Leave me alone," was all she said.

He didn't say anything, and for a moment she wondered if the call had been dropped, but then she heard James's quiet laughter, the kind that sent goose bumps up her arms and fear deep into her soul.

"I mean it, James. Leave me alone."

"Who's the guy?"

It took her a moment to figure out what he meant. "My new boss."

"Oh, yeah?"

"It doesn't matter who he is. You're out of my life, remember? Gone. And if you don't leave me alone, I'm going to call every news station in town and have them do a story about ex-boyfriends who stalk their ex-girlfriends after they beat the crap out of them."

Silence.

She'd never threatened to go public before. She hadn't even told Colt and Natalie about the abuse until she'd gotten out of the hospital. And she'd downplayed the seriousness of the matter. It wasn't until James had shown up at the ranch one day that she'd come clean to Colt. In hindsight, it must have been shortly after James's visit that Colt had thought of the idea of putting his brother in charge.

James laughed. "If you do that, I'll sue you for defamation of character."

"You could try," she said. "But your mug shot is online. Kinda hard to call me a liar when the proof of your guilt is on the internet for all to see." He didn't respond, and his silence gave her courage. "So unless you want to be this week's special feature, I suggest you give me a wide berth from here on out, got it?"

"My, my, my. Someone's grown some claws. Wonder if it has anything to do with the new man in your life."

"You're right. I do have claws. Hello Kitty claws. And I'll use them on you if you don't leave me alone."

"Are you seeing him?"

"I'm not dating anyone. Not now. Not ever. I'm done

with men. Most of all, I'm done with you. Now leave me alone, or I swear to the good Lord, you'll be sorry."

She hung up before he could ignite her temper any more.

"I take it that was James?"

Chance leaned against the trailer door. Wow. That must have been the world's shortest shower. "I called him," she said. "Told him to leave me alone."

"And you think he'll listen?"

"If he has any sense he will. I threatened to out him on television if he didn't."

He nodded, his hair still wet, as was hers, but she'd bet he looked ten times better than she did. He looked as though he'd come from a photo shoot, one of those sexy-men-out-of-the-shower shoots, complete with white T-shirt clinging to his damp skin and skintight jeans.

"We should probably turn in." He stood back so she could enter the trailer. "Long day tomorrow."

And she would have to sleep by him. This would be a long night.

Chapter Eight

When Chance woke up the next morning, he'd have been the first one to admit his bad mood. Sleep deprivation did that to a man, especially when the lack of sleep involved a woman.

Who wasn't in the trailer.

He checked the bathroom. And the bed where she'd slept, the same damn bed he'd thought about crawling into last night, even though he knew she'd kick him out if he did.

I'm not dating anyone. Not now. Not ever.

Her words should have served as a stern reminder why he should steer clear. Instead they were like a call to arms, at least as far as his body was concerned. He couldn't stop thinking about her.

Where was she?

The trailer wasn't that big, and since she wasn't inside, she must be outside, after he'd specifically told her not to leave without him.

Damn it.

He burst outside so fast he knocked the trailer door open all the way, its boom no doubt startling their neighbor.

"There you are," he said, grimacing slightly at the accusatory sound of his words. "Where were you?"

"Sorry," she said, somehow looking five years younger in her bulky sweatshirt and ponytail. "I thought I would feed the horses."

"And I thought I told you to stay put."

"You did, but I made sure the coast was clear. And just in case, I brought my kitty claws and my pepper spray." She held both up, then put them back in her pockets. "Even if James had shown up, I would have been okay."

"Famous last words."

"No. Really."

How could he make her see things through his eyes? It was the most frustrating part of this whole situation.

"Carolina, I'm serious. Once, when I was over there, in the Middle East, we found a woman huddling behind some bushes. Strangest thing we'd ever come across way out in the middle of nowhere. At first we thought she might be some kind of radical Islamist—you never know these days—but we took one look at her face and knew she was no terrorist."

He stepped toward her, hoping she'd see the utter seriousness in his eyes.

"She'd been beaten by her husband. Guess he took offense to some other man trying to talk to her. Blamed it on her, and so she ran."

Her face paled. "You don't have to tell me any more."

"Yes, I do. I need you to understand something about the opposite sex, something that not a lot of women know, but that I saw firsthand. There are men out there who think they own their wives or girlfriends—I mean, *own* own. They look upon women as a commodity. As a thing. It was bad over there. Worse than you can possibly imagine. This poor woman was married to such a man. We tried to get her some help. Tried to take her to our embassy. Asylum. Whatever you want to call it. Didn't do a damn bit of good. The sons of bitches wouldn't let us help her. We had to turn her over to her own people. We heard later that she'd been beaten to death the next day."

"Oh, Chance. I'm sorry."

He shook his head. "Don't be sorry for me. Be sorry for that woman. You have a choice, Caro. You can either stick with me and be safe, or you can go trotting off on your own and put yourself at risk. After what I saw over there, I don't trust any man that puts his hands on a woman. James is no exception."

She nodded. "Okay. I get it."

"I hope you do."

"I was coming back to change. I want to put Rio through his paces. He's still pretty green, and I'm not sure what he'll be like in this arena."

Rio. Her new stunt horse. He'd watched her practice this past week, marveling at her ability. She was by far and away the best trick rider of the Galloping Girlz, doing things no sane woman should do, like standing on the shoulders of one of the other girls, a stunt he'd never seen before. But no matter how brave she was, she'd be no match for James.

"I'll watch," he offered because there was no way he wanted her walking to the arena without him. It was bad enough he'd somehow missed her getting up to feed the horses. If he were honest, he wasn't angry at her so much as at himself.

"You don't have to do that."

"Go change," he offered by way of response. "I'll wait outside."

Damn lack of sleep. It made him edgy. And impatient. And cranky.

But she didn't leave right away. She held eye contact, her eyes seeming to be as blue as the wild lilac that bloomed in the spring. It was still too early for direct sunlight, but she didn't need light to shine. A piece of hay stuck in her hair. He told himself to ignore it, but instead he reached for it, slowly, so as not to scare her.

"Thank you," she said softly, but he didn't know if she thanked him for wanting to keep her safe or for removing the piece of hay.

"You're welcome."

She entered the trailer and closed the door softly. Chance backed up a step and collapsed into a camp chair he'd set up outside. This attraction thing needed to stop. In a couple months, three at most, he'd be overseas again. Plus, he'd heard her earlier. *I'm done with men*, she'd said. *Never again.*

Bad timing. Bad idea. Bad choice.

He was a combat veteran, one who took his career seriously, and he needed to stick to the mission—protecting her.

The trailer door opened, and she paused for a moment. She'd changed into a skintight leotard, one with a silver swath of fabric that ran up her leg, intersected her middle and ended at her shoulder. It left nothing to the imagination. Again.

Damn.

He stood up quickly. "Let's go."

She didn't say a word, simply fell into step beside him. It took her only a moment to tack up Rio—the horse's special saddle so light it looked as if it required hardly any effort to lift onto Rio's back. Off-white in color, the saddle was smaller and flatter in the back and, yes, had a saddle horn, but it was tiny compared to a normal saddle.

"Arena could be crowded," he observed as she slipped on Rio's bridle.

"That's okay. There's always people around."

It was early morning, and a crispness hung in the air, typical of mountain rodeos. But the time and temperature didn't stop people from wandering about. Slack—a section of the rodeo not attended by the general public—would start in an hour or so. Most competitors currently tended to their horses, though a few were already riding.

Chance scanned the perimeter and sidelines for anyone who might look suspicious, but there was nobody. Everyone was on horseback, which helped eliminate potential threats, unless...

"Does James ride?" he asked.

Carolina huffed in laughter as she opened the arena gate. "Hardly."

He nodded and then peered up at the grandstand. Nobody there, either. He wished he had his scope. The pine trees surrounding them would make a great hiding place.

You're being paranoid.

Maybe he was, but her conversation with James had put Chance on edge. It hadn't sounded very friendly, and it made him think this thing between them was far from over.

"I won't take long," she said, swinging up on Rio's back with the ease of a ballerina. "Colt will be here later, and he'll want to go through the whole routine with me and the girls."

And Chance would get to watch. That was fine. He

liked to be in the background, keeping an eye on things. Like now. If James showed up, the man would be in for a surprise. And it wouldn't be just him jumping the man. He would bet a half a dozen cowboys would come to Carolina's rescue if anything were to happen. You didn't mess with women at rodeos—not if you valued your life. More importantly, you didn't mess with his woman.

His?

Well, not like that, he reassured himself. Not *ever* like that.

Caro set off on Rio, nodding and waving to the cowboys she passed, blond ponytail bouncing up and down in rhythm to her horse. Everyone knew her. That removed some of the tension from his shoulders. More friendlies meant fewer potential hostiles to keep an eye on. Chance scanned every face in the arena, all the while watching as Caro brought Rio up to speed. It was hard to keep his eyes off her once she began her tricks.

She amazed him.

He couldn't watch her hang upside down without feeling his stomach drop somewhere near his toes—the same feeling he got when he jumped out of a plane. And yet, he marveled. If he saw the move a million times, he'd never grow tired of it. Her hair whipped around as furiously as her horse's tail while she performed her repertoire of tricks. When she stood up on Rio's back, it was almost anticlimactic. Easy. Not much of a challenge compared to galloping upside down with nothing more than a single leg hooked around the breast collar.

POP.

Chance flinched. Caro's horse bolted.

"Caro." He jumped over the fence so fast he damn near tripped on the top rail. Caro had somehow managed to clutch the back of the saddle, but her legs hung down, her lower body flopping about. She might have been okay except Rio wasn't a seasoned trick horse. Spooked, he started to buck. Hard.

Dear God.

Caro's grip slipped. He could hear her yelling, "Whoa, Rio, whoa," but it did little good. One of the cowboys in the arena turned his horse and galloped toward her, but it was too little too late. Like a rag doll tossed by a petulant kid, Caro flew through the air, arms splayed, legs akimbo. She landed with an audible thud that twisted his gut.

"Caro!"

She didn't move, and it sent him into a panic he'd never felt before. Not when he'd been caught in a firefight. Not when he'd spotted that IED six inches from his left foot. Not when that shell blast had knocked him back on his keister.

"Caro." He all but threw himself down. "Can you hear me?"

She groaned.

"Caro."

She muttered something, and he leaned in close to hear it.

"I'm going to kill that horse."

He drew back quickly. Blue eyes met his own.

"Don't worry. I'll do it for you."

She nodded, winced and clutched her head.

"Are you hurt?"

"Just banged up, I think."

"Stay still while we wait for the EMTs to arrive."

"EMTs? I don't need an EMT." She slowly sat up, a clod of dirt falling off the front of her shirt.

"I said don't move."

"I'm fine." She waved him back.

Dirt covered her leotard and her face and was in her hair. "You are not fine."

"I've survived worse." She started to stand.

"Carolina Cruthers, you are not to move another inch until an EMT has checked you out!"

He'd never yelled at a woman before, but there was a first for everything. His words had the desired effect. She froze in place and stared up at him.

"Jeez," she said, eyes wide. "I got bucked off my horse. No big deal."

He shook his head, trying to convey the seriousness of his words. "You weren't just bucked off. You were shot."

Chapter Nine

Caro thought she'd misheard him.

"Excuse me?"

"I heard a gunshot just as Rio started to buck."

Shot.

She jumped to her feet.

"Hey!"

She ignored him. *Rio.*

She didn't know the man who had come up alongside of the gelding, leaned over and caught the reins. She ran toward him and Rio, searching the horse for blood, for a limp, for some sign of injury.

"Caro!"

She didn't stop, despite her aching foot and shoulders. Plus, she was pretty certain she'd have a massive bruise on her hip tomorrow. She ignored it all because if Rio had been shot...

"You okay?" the cowboy who held Rio's reins asked. The man, who seemed vaguely familiar, stared down at her with a look of concern and kindness.

"Fine." Her words came out in a rush, as if she could slow down time by speeding up her words. "Easy, Rio."

She placed her hands against his brown coat. He'd begun to sweat, his bay color stained a darker shade.

His veins were distended. His sides expanded and contracted quickly. *Shock?* A quick scan didn't reveal any noticeable injuries. Maybe Chance had been wrong—

There.

On the point of his butt, right next to his tail, a small swelling.

"Do you see anything?"

She glanced at Chance, who had come up behind her. She saw the worry in his eyes. She pointed to Rio's injury in response, moving in for a closer look. It had started to swell, but there was no blood. No hole, either, where the bullet might have gone in. In fact, the wound looked more like a bee sting than a bullet wound.

"Are you sure he was shot?"

"Shot?" said the man who still held Rio's reins. "Are you serious?"

"I thought I heard something, too," said another cowboy. "A *crack* right as her horse started to bolt."

"Must have startled him," surmised the first man, tipping the brim of his straw hat. "That's why he started to buck."

"No," Chance said. "He was shot *at.*"

"Shot at?" the cowboy said in disbelief. "As in someone fired a bullet at him?" He shook his head. "No one's going to shoot at a horse, not at a rodeo."

Carolina tried to remain calm. A person would do that if he were angry because she'd broken up with him. If he wanted to hurt her because she'd dared to go to the police. If he were enraged because she'd threatened to publicize what he'd done to her.

"There's no bullet hole," said one of the men.

"No, there's not," she mused, turning toward Chance in question.

"Because he wasn't shot with a rifle." Chance's gaze encompassed them all. "It was an air gun. I could hear the hiss of the cartridge when it discharged."

"You some kind of gun expert, then?" the man in the straw hat asked.

Chance nodded. "I was an Army Ranger. Combat active. Discharged two weeks ago."

That shut the man up, and it explained a lot to Caro, too. That's why Rio was swollen and not bleeding. The bump was a welt. She straightened suddenly as a new thought penetrated.

Did James watch them?

"He's gone," Chance said, placing a hand on her shoulder. "There's no way he'd stick around, not after watching you get back up. He knows you're okay."

"Which means he might be back."

"I don't think he wants you dead." He shook his head. "It's like I said. Some men can't take rejection. But James is not stupid. He just wants to see you scared."

"Someone trying to hurt you?" asked the cowboy.

James had already hurt her. And now he'd hurt her again. And almost her horse. She wanted to cry, except she didn't. She took a deep breath and said, "My ex."

The answer seemed to satisfy the man, because he pulled the brim of his hat down low, as if preparing to face someone on a most-wanted poster. "If someone's trying to hurt you, Carolina, I'll tell a few of the boys. Nobody will get near this arena again. Not without us checking them out."

"What about tonight?" she asked. "What about when Slack starts in an hour or so? What about when I perform?" And as she said the words, emotion built inside her. "He's not going to stop just because people are around. He's insane. Crazy." Just like Chance had said he was.

And he'd tried to hurt her horse.

Funny how you could go around blaming yourself. How you could deal with someone doling out punches. Live with it, even, but when that same someone tried to injure an animal you loved...

She looked at Chance. "I'll be right back."

"Where are you going?"

Pain shot up her leg as she turned away, but she didn't care. Rio could have been hurt from that shot, no matter that it was a rubber bullet, a pellet or whatever kind of projectile James had used. If it'd hit Rio in the wrong spot—the eye, maybe.

"I'm calling the police." She paused, turned back to face the men. "And then I'm going to call the local media. And then I'm going to hire a hit man to kill that son of a bitch."

Chance's brow lifted. It brought the edge of his cowboy hat up, so she could perfectly see the play of emotion in his eyes. Surprise. Dismay. Mostly though, she spotted approval.

"Attagirl."

CHANCE SMILED. She was true to her word, not that any of her calls amounted to much of anything.

"We'll have an extra patrol run by the rodeo grounds tonight," said a black-clad officer who didn't look old enough to shave, much less own a gun. "In the meantime, I'll call VDC PD and see what they can do on their end."

Carolina nodded at the young officer. "Anything you can do to help."

Help? This kid didn't know how to help. He'd probably never discharged his weapon anywhere other than the firing range, much less in the line of duty. Yet Caro appeared to be strangely reassured by the man's words.

It irritated the heck out of Chance.

"What's going on here?"

They both turned, and Chance was relieved to see his brother. "Something wrong?" Colt asked.

Chance had tried to call him earlier, but he'd only gotten Colt's voice mail, and he refused to leave messages when someone was driving.

"James shot my horse," Carolina stated.

"What?" Colt glanced between them. "Is Rio okay?"

"He's fine," Chance answered. "It was an Airsoft rifle, probably. Rubber pellet. We found it after searching for an hour. Rio has a welt the size of a grapefruit on his rear. He'll be fine. When we get back to the ranch tomorrow, I'll have Ethan take a look at it to be certain, but I'm pretty sure it's just bruised."

His future brother-in-law, Ethan, was a veterinarian. He'd know what to do, and that made her feel a little bit better.

"That does it," Colt said, looking as angry as a stepped-on rooster. He jerked his hat off his head. "That son of a bitch is going down."

"We've got things handled, sir," said the kid cop.

Colt ignored him. "Carolina, on Monday I'm taking you straight down to the courthouse and you're filing suit against him. I don't know what you can charge him with, but something's got to be better than nothing."

"Don't worry. I plan to do more than that," Caro said, hands on her hips.

Chance suspected James had crossed an invisible line

with her. Good. She needed to realize this was a serious matter. He hadn't been kidding when he'd said men could do horrible things to women they professed to love.

"In the meantime, Chance, you're not to leave her side." His brother's gaze fell on him.

Chance cocked a thumb at Carolina. "Tell her that."

"I know," she said, her face grim. "I'm sorry. Chance has been trying to keep an eye on me, but I didn't want to be a bother. Believe me, I'll be more careful now."

"And I'll be more alert."

Chance was mad at himself for taking his eyes off their surroundings. For watching Caro as she practiced. He should have scouted the perimeter before she rode. Should have insisted she forgo practicing. It wasn't as though she didn't know the routine. She could have sat out one practice session, but he never would have thought James...

"She could have been killed falling off her horse," Colt said the same thing he'd been thinking.

And if Caro had been seriously injured, he would never have forgiven himself. As it was, he felt a deep, rolling rage. James had clearly wanted her to be bucked off, and something else, too.

Chance stroked his jaw. Something about the whole situation was off. He couldn't quite put his finger on it, but it was the same kind of feeling he got when a group of insurgents showed up at a strange and obscure location. There was always a method to a crazy man's madness.

"I think it's safe to say your assailant won't be back," said the baby boy in blue—an Officer Walker. "Men like him usually run scared after they've made a move."

Chance tried not to laugh. As if Officer Walker had

been on the force long enough to make that assumption. However, Chance would bet the cop was right. There were enough cowboys and cowgirls pissed off about the whole thing that James would be stupid to try something again. Too many people on alert now.

"Here's the plan," Chance said to the group, splaying his hand in Caro's direction. "You're not performing tonight. Delilah can take your place."

"What?" Caro's mouth dropped open. She looked toward his brother as if he could help change Chance's mind, and that irritated Chance all the more.

"She doesn't know the new routine," Chance added, "but she can figure it out. She's watched you enough times."

"My brother's right," Colt said. "We can't take any chances. You're grounded until further notice, and you—" he turned to Chance "—you're going to stick to her like glue. I'll sleep in Bill's trailer tonight. I don't want any gossip starting about a single girl sharing a trailer with two men. You and Caro can take mine again."

It quickly became clear that Caro wasn't just mad, she was livid. Two hours later, as the crowd cheered in the distance for the Galloping Girlz and their new routine, Caro prowled around the interior of the trailer like one of the military dogs his sister cared for.

"This is ridiculous," she said after pacing across the length of the trailer for the tenth time. "There's a million people out there. James wouldn't dare try and pull something tonight."

"Just the same, you're staying in here."

"What about tomorrow?" She shook her head in aggravation, her blond hair flying over her shoulders. "Am I supposed to sit around all day?"

"Think of it as a vacation."

"I should go home."

"And be at the ranch all by yourself? I don't think so."

She released an oath of frustration. "Natalie would be there."

Her eyes implored him to see reason. Wasn't going to work.

"And your sister's not far away," she added.

He shook his head, emphatically so she got the point. "I'm not willing to jeopardize their safety because you're bored."

She drew up short. Clearly, she hadn't thought that far ahead. A second later, she flounced down on the couch opposite him.

"I can't stand being pent up like this."

He reached behind him and stretched his arms. "Then do something productive with all that energy."

"Like what?"

It was one of those things—a suggestion he hadn't known he was going to propose, and something he probably shouldn't mention. "Training."

She cocked a brow at him, and with her hair down and loose around her shoulders and her black T-shirt clinging to her every curve, he began to doubt the soundness of his suggestion. He should be keeping away from her, not planting ideas in her head.

"What do you mean?" she asked when he failed to explain.

Don't do it. Do not do it. You know how uncomfortable she makes you feel. Touching her will only complicate matters. He'd had enough fantasies about her last night.

"Self-defense."

The voice inside his head groaned, but he couldn't ignore the fact that she needed training. Pepper spray only went so far. If that bastard ex of hers was crazy enough to shoot at her horse, no telling what else he would do. And if he ever caught her off guard, if he managed to surprise her one night at the ranch, she wouldn't have time to get out her spray or arm herself with a weapon. Today was proof of that. So if Chance taught her a few of the moves he'd learned in the army, she might have a fighting chance.

"You should learn to protect yourself."

Oh, yeah? asked the voice. *Who's going to protect you?*

"You mean learn karate or something?"

"You don't need karate. There's a lot you can do with just your hands."

And if he needed proof of what a bad idea this whole thing was, those words sure did seal the deal, because there was a lot she could do with her hands…and he wished she'd do it all to him.

Chapter Ten

She should have said no.

Later that evening, Carolina wondered what the hell she'd gotten herself into. At least, she'd been granted a momentary reprieve. She had been downright embarrassed earlier. When the girls had returned, Lori had banged on the door, shouting, "Whadda ya guys doing in there?"

Carolina had wanted to die. Despite telling Chance she didn't care what everyone thought, she didn't want to be thought of as a floozy – shacking up with the boss's brother. Although word would spread quickly that she had an issue with an ex, so she probably had nothing to worry about.

"Now, remember, you're never going to win if you're facing a man with a gun."

They stood between the two trailers, in an area shielded from people passing by, the grass in between them trampled from their feet.

"I know," she said, nervously tucking her hands into her pockets.

"The best thing to do if that happens is run. But not straight. Zigzag. Do the unexpected. And dive behind something if you can."

She nodded. It was late. The rodeo had ended long ago. Colt had gone off to tend to the horses. The girls had fled somewhere else…probably to the local bar. That left her and Chance alone, the sun at an angle that lit the tops of the trees on fire, the sky a yellow orange that would have taken her breath away if she wasn't already breathing hard in anticipation of what they were about to do. It was ridiculous. It wasn't as though Chance would hurt her. He was going to teach her to keep from being hurt.

"The first thing I'm going to teach you is how to deflect a punch."

Whoo boy. That was training she could have used a while ago. And it was crazy, because merely thinking about that night made the lip James had split in two hurt. The memory was so powerful it was all she could do not to run away. Her heart ran away instead.

Despite her feelings, Carolina held her ground. Damn that James. Damn any man that would try and hurt her.

"Do I use my arms?" It was what she'd done the night James attacked her. She had lifted her arms and used them to cover her face…

"No. Not quite. But first things first. If someone comes at you this way—" Chance stepped in her direction, and she flinched slightly, which was ridiculous, because she didn't have anything to fear from Chance. His eyes narrowed.

"I'm not going to hurt you," he said quietly.

"I know."

He stared at her in concern, and it made her breath catch just as it had yesterday. How could a man be such a warrior on the outside and so warm and tender on the inside?

Chance tilted his head. "If this brings back too many memories, we can stop."

"No. I need to learn this."

"Good," he said. "Because if you listen to me closely, from here on out, you'll be the one in control. No one will ever hit you again, I promise."

She looked down at the ground to hide her eyes. Despite her earlier anger, she wanted to cry again, and she hated that. She was not the crying type. Never had been. Never would be. And yet somehow, she'd become Pitiful Pearl—in the flesh—and damned if she knew how she'd gotten that way.

She sucked in a deep breath. "Okay. Show me again."

For the longest time, his eyes roved over her face, as if trying to decide if he should trust her words.

"Bend your arms up like this," he said at last. "Like a crossing guard holding a sign."

She followed his instructions.

"Good. Now. When I come at you—" he stepped even closer "—you move your arm like I showed you. Are you ready?"

Another deep breath, one that seemed to stoke the fires of determination in her heart. She could do this. She was not the sniveling ninny James had reduced her to. She could trust this man.

"Ready?"

He swung a fist in her direction. She deflected it. Easily. Quickly.

"Good job."

And the victory she felt, the euphoria at deflecting his swing, made her feel—well, she couldn't help but smile. It felt good to take charge.

"Do it again," she told him.

He swung once more, faster. She moved quicker this time, and the maneuver worked the same way. So easy. So simple. With practice she probably wouldn't have to think about it.

"That was great," she said. Never again would she find herself cowering before a man, letting him hit her, being afraid for her life.

Chance smiled his approval, and she thought it was a crying shame no woman had caught his interest. With his masculine skills and easy smile, half her teammates wanted to go after him. Half of Natalie's clients seemed enamored with him, too. She didn't blame them.

"Now," he continued, "sometimes people will try and grab you when they realize you can deflect a punch. I'm going to teach you some pressure points that will help deter anyone who tries to grab you. The first one is here." He pointed to his wrist. "Right above the bone. If you dig your thumb in, you'll bring a man down. Trust me." He offered her his arm, motioning for her to try it.

"I don't want to hurt you."

"It's okay. I'm going to swing again, only this time when you deflect, I'll grab you, too. You clutch my wrist and press as hard as you can where I showed you."

For some reason, she crouched. He grinned, and she had the inexplicable urge to do something crazy—like laugh. Instead she waited.

He came at her fast. She deflected. He grabbed. She pressed. *Hard.*

"Ow, ow, ow." He dropped to the ground. She released immediately. He sucked in a breath.

Carolina gulped. "Oh, my goodness. Did I hurt you?" She closed the distance between them. When he stood and bent his head to examine his wrist, they were only inches away.

"No, I'm good. You just surprised me, is all."

He looked up at the same time she did, and they were face-to-face, his breath on hers and her breath on him. His eyes peered down at her so softly, she couldn't believe how it felt to have him there, next to her. Exciting. Reassuring. Peaceful.

"Well, good," she mumbled. "I'm glad." She looked away, because her heart had begun to beat so hard she was sure he could see it. Or maybe he heard it thundering in her ears.

"Okay. Yeah. Well." He stepped back. "There's one more maneuver I'd like to show you."

He clenched his hands, and she wondered if he'd felt it, too, that moment when the ground beneath her feet seemed to slide off the side of the earth and it was all she could do not to hang on.

To him.

She wanted to hold him.

"Turn around," he said.

Did he still feel it, she hoped, as she blindly followed his instructions. And then he was there, right there, up behind her, and she could feel the heat of him and she almost groaned.

Oh, holy hell.

She bolted. Spun. Faced him.

"What?" His expression was bewildered.

She didn't know *what*. Something crazy was going on, because she was never going to let a man get close to her again, not even one as nice as Chance.

"I heard a bee," she lied.

He chuckled. "No bees. Just me."

It was no use getting attached to Chance. He was leaving soon. Colt had told her a half-dozen times that Chance would only be Stateside long enough to witness the birth of another nephew or niece. Then he was gone. So even if she did like his smile and the kindness in his eyes and the way he made her feel safe and protected, it was temporary.

"Go on," he urged. "Turn around."

She didn't want to. She didn't, but she had no choice. He came up behind her again, and everything around them retreated. The two trailers side by side. The people walking by on the road. The horses and dogs that wandered the rodeo grounds. Everything.

"You don't need to be afraid," he whispered into her ear.

She wasn't afraid. Not even a little.

"I promise not to hurt you."

No. He would never do that. She knew that with every fiber of her being.

"This is what you do if someone grabs you from behind."

She tensed because she knew he would touch her, and a second later, his hands were on her shoulders and she almost gasped.

"They'll probably wrap their arms around you." His hands slid down. She smelled his clean scent—a combination of talc and citrus—and it caused her to close her eyes.

"You'll never break free by trying to use your hands."

No. She'd learned that lesson the hard way. The thought was a sobering one, and it caused her to sharpen her focus.

"The first thing you do is insert your foot between my legs."

She did as instructed, which meant their legs touched. Her sharpness faded again at the feel of his rock-hard limbs. *Oh, dear goodness.*

"Now, take your elbow and jab it into my ribs."

"But I—"

"Do it."

She jabbed. Hard.

The breath gushed out of him. The scent of him faded as he moved away slightly.

"Good," he wheezed. "Now, this next time, take a step back. So it's leg between, jab and step back. All in one move. Then as he's falling backward, slip down and out of my arms." He closed the distance again, wrapped an arm around her neck. "Quickly. Do it."

She hesitated.

"Now."

She jabbed. He grunted again. She thrust herself back. They both went down.

"Whoa," he cried, somehow shifting so she landed on top of him. "You forgot the leg."

They lay belly to belly, breath to breath, and his eyes were full of amusement and something else. Something that made her whole world tilt and her heart soften.

"I'm sorry."

"Don't be." He tucked a stray piece of hair behind her ear. "You're doing great."

Everything warmed. Her face. Her skin where they touched. Even...

She rolled away. "I'm no good at this."

"You will be." He sat up. "It just takes practice."

She wasn't talking about self-defense. She was talking about *her*. About her disastrous past. About how she seemed to pick the wrong man or the right man at the wrong time. She met his gaze, and she knew he was the latter. Any woman could see that, even someone as messed up as her.

"Hey," he said, clearly reading her distress. "It's okay. You'll catch on."

"I don't think I'm cut out for this. My mom—"

She stopped herself, but he'd caught the words.

"What about your mom?"

She shook her head.

He scooted closer, using a single finger to turn her chin so she faced him.

"What about your mom?"

Carolina hated the fact she'd brought her up. That she was somehow blaming her for her troubles. She'd never been one to point the finger at anyone but herself, and she wasn't about to start now. Still, Carolina couldn't escape the need for the truth in his eyes, and she needed to tell him, if only so he would understand how messed up she was.

"She wasn't the best role model in the world."

"No?"

"Apparently, I've learned a lot from her."

That was an understatement. Different men all the time. Some were nice. Some were kind. Some were old and wanted things no man twice her age should want, not from her.

"Don't blame yourself for James."

"He's exactly the kind of man my mom would bring home."

"And he's gone from your life."

"Not yet."

"But he will be."

Would he? These days it seemed as though the bad guys were in and out of jail faster than someone could change a tire. And if that happened, if James was arrested for assault and he went to jail and then got out on bail the next day, presuming he would even make it to jail, what then? Who would protect her then? Chance would be long gone. The district attorney had told her it'd be months before James went to trial. Suddenly, Carolina wished with all her might that Chance wasn't going to leave.

"Hey." He must have read the fear in her eyes because his eyes softened. "It'll be okay."

It would not. Nothing would ever be okay again. She had only to look into his eyes to know that.

Carolina had fallen for the wrong guy. Again.

Chapter Eleven

He wanted to kiss her.

With her eyes searching his, imploring, it was all he could do not to lean down and plant his lips on hers. He couldn't. Wouldn't. Shouldn't.

She blinked. He did, too, and the momentary break in eye contact was enough. He stood, held out a hand.

"Let's practice some more," he said.

She nodded, blond hair falling over one shoulder. She was so tiny. Too small to defend herself against a man like James, at least not without any self-defense training. That James had struck her, that he still taunted her—well, it started a fire inside Chance's heart, one that he focused on instead of how appealing she looked at that moment.

She took his outstretched hand. He pulled her to her feet, and she landed against him.

God.

If she had any idea how aroused he was with her against him, well, she'd probably call off the rest of their lesson.

"Remember," he said into her ear. "Step, wedge, thrust."

He didn't give her time to comment, simply wrapped

an arm around her. She didn't hesitate this time, planting her leg between his own, thrusting back and using such force he didn't need to fake falling down.

Damn, he loved the way her eyes lit up with triumph. "That was easy," she said.

"Let's do it again."

It was a form of physical torture. He came up behind her, his body buzzing and warming in places he wouldn't acknowledge. She thrust her leg through his own—bringing to mind other things she could do with her legs—then shifted back up against him, her rear end coming into contact with his midsection, which made him groan.

She froze. "Did I hurt you?"

Not in the way she thought. "I'm fine. Just keep going."

She thrust back. He dropped to the ground, and he couldn't take any more. It wasn't like him to quit, but there was no shame in knowing your own weak spots. Caro Cruthers was definitely a weak spot.

"I think we should call it a night."

It was a good time to do exactly that. The sun had dropped low, and they were quickly losing daylight. Soon the shadows would deepen, and he'd rather be inside when that happened.

Inside. With Caro.

It was a thought that repeated itself as they readied for the night. He managed to distract himself for a bit by cooking dinner, but all too soon it was time to turn in.

"Thanks," she said, standing by the bedroom doorway. "Really, Chance. I appreciate all you're doing to help me."

"Think nothing of it," he said, turning away, having

to turn away, because if she stared across at him with her big blue eyes one more time he'd…

What?

He didn't know, but he didn't want to find out.

"Good night," she said, closing the bedroom door.

Son of a—

Don't think about it. Don't think about the fact that right now she's on the other side of that door, stripping out of her clothes, tugging tiny little panties down over her hips.

You don't even know if she wears panties.

That was the problem, he told himself. He had no business wanting to find out.

He gazed out the trailer window. As he had so many times before, he told himself to focus on the job at hand. He doubted that bastard James would try anything. Not tonight. He knew they were on to him. After he'd shot Rio, the putz had probably headed back to Via Del Caballo, which is where they should be tonight.

Chance sighed. He should have used Colt's truck and taken her home. But no. She'd insisted on sticking around, wanting to be there for the team despite not performing.

He busied himself with work. He had a new job, and DTS had forms for him to fill out. Fortunately, he could do much of it through his smartphone. There were emails to answer, too, notes from his former combat buddies. Messages on social media from people he'd met over the years. He had no idea how long he'd been on the couch when he heard a noise. It came from the other side of the door.

Carolina.

She groaned, a groan of fear, pain and anguish.

Ignore her.

She cried out again, and against his better judgment, he crossed to the door and opened it slightly. A light outside the trailer perfectly illuminated her face. Her blond hair contrasted with the dark brown pillows.

Nothing would have convinced him to take the bed. The bed was for her, he'd insisted, especially since her body still ached from being bucked from Rio. Chance had been grateful when she hadn't argued. He needed a door between them.

"No!" Carolina flinched. His stomach sank to his toes. She was probably dreaming of James.

How could someone hit a woman? He'd never understood the need to beat someone who couldn't defend herself.

Carolina's head swung left, then right, as if she fought off blows in her dreams.

Damn it.

He didn't want to. He really didn't, but he couldn't stop from entering her room. The bed was above the hitch of the trailer, which meant there was no way for him to walk along the side of the bed. All he could do was use his voice.

But, man, did he want to touch her.

He couldn't believe how badly he fought the urge. He wanted to crawl up beside her, brush the fear from her face with his fingers, ease the pain of her cries and tell her everything was all right. Nothing would happen to her.

She flung an arm up, but then she quieted and he continued to watch.

He needed to leave. He turned before he could convince himself to do otherwise, but he didn't stop at the couch. No. He burst into the cool night air before he could think better of it. There were chairs out in front. He settled into one of them. Wouldn't be the first time he'd kept watch outside. And sitting in a canvas director's chair sure beat propping himself up against a rock. He tipped his cowboy hat down and closed his eyes.

It was the last thing he remembered.

When he opened his eyes, Caro stood in front of him, holding out a mug. He shot up in surprise, but not even scrubbing a hand over his face helped to clear his mind. *Son of a—*

He must have conked out. That wasn't like him. Not when he was on watch.

"Here." She waved the mug in front of her. "You look like you need this."

He took the steaming cup from her, knowing a big sip of caffeine wouldn't shake the cobwebs from his mind. "Sorry," he said. "I had meant to keep watch, maybe get a little shut-eye, but not sleep until dawn."

She smiled. "Busy day yesterday."

"That's for sure." He took a sip of the coffee, wincing at its strength.

"What's wrong?" Her blue eyes widened with concern, and he marveled that she could read him so easily.

"Strong."

"Sorry. I usually get the dark roast."

"I'll go get some sugar."

"No, no. I'll get it. I think there's some inside."

"Stay," he said, standing. "I saw it last night when I was cooking."

He didn't give her an opportunity to respond. He needed to get up and stretch his legs. Inside the trailer,

FREE Merchandise is 'in the Cards' for you!

Dear Reader,

We're giving away FREE MERCHANDISE!

Seriously, we'd like to reward you for reading this novel by giving you **FREE MERCHANDISE** worth over **$20** retail. And no purchase is necessary!

You see the Jack of Hearts sticker above? Paste that sticker in the box on the Free Merchandise Voucher inside. Return the Voucher promptly...and we'll send you valuable Free Merchandise!

Thanks again for reading one of our novels—and enjoy your Free Merchandise with our compliments!

Pam Powers

Pam Powers

P.S. Look inside to see what Free Merchandise is **"in the cards"** for you!

We'd like to send you two free books like the one you are enjoying now. Your two books have a combined price of over $10 retail, but they are yours to keep absolutely FREE! We'll even send you 2 wonderful surprise gifts. You can't lose!

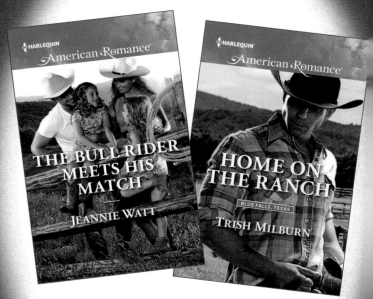

REMEMBER: Your Free Merchandise, consisting of **2 Free Books** and **2 Free Gifts**, is worth over $20 retail! No purchase is necessary, so please send for your Free Merchandise today.

Get TWO FREE GIFTS!
We'll also send you 2 wonderful FREE GIFTS (worth about $10 retail), in addition to your 2 Free books!

Visit us at:
www.ReaderService.com

Books received may not be as shown.

BUSINESS REPLY MAIL
FIRST-CLASS MAIL   PERMIT NO. 717   BUFFALO, NY

POSTAGE WILL BE PAID BY ADDRESSEE

READER SERVICE
PO BOX 1867
BUFFALO NY 14240-9952

NO POSTAGE
NECESSARY
IF MAILED
IN THE
UNITED STATES

Chance headed to a cabinet to the left of the sink. The sugar was right where he remembered.

He heard a noise outside.

The hairs stood up on the back of his neck. He didn't usually get such strong premonitions, but when he did…

He set the mug down on the counter, turned and ran for the door.

"Let me go!"

Chance froze, but only for a split second because his instincts had proved right. James. He jumped off the steps at the same time Caro used one of the maneuvers he'd taught her yesterday, the one that allowed you to twist away from someone who'd grabbed your arm. James, a big hulk of a guy, tried for her again.

"Hey!"

James glanced at him, and Chance plowed into him with everything he had.

Oomph.

James might be big, but he didn't have years of combat experience. He didn't know there was a pressure point on the side of the neck that would send spasms through your whole body and make you cry out in pain.

"Don't move," Chance said, easing the pressure, but only a bit.

"My neck." Big paws tried to swipe him away.

"I *said*, don't move." More pressure, more cries of pain, but the hands dropped.

"Caro, call the police."

She ran into the trailer to get her cell phone.

Enraged gray eyes met his own. James might be big, but his eyes were tiny. His lips were thin, though that could be because he grimaced in pain. Still, Chance didn't know what Caro had seen in the man. She could do so much better.

"I'm going to let you up." He released the pressure again. "Slowly."

James didn't move. Not when Chance slipped off him and not when someone—Chance didn't know who—appeared and asked, "Need any help?" Chance wasn't sure who the man meant—him or James. Chance glanced around. Other people were coming out of their trailers.

"You broke my neck," James said.

"I didn't." Chance stood.

James groaned. "My whole body feels numb."

"It's just a nerve. It'll come back."

Silver eyes snarled at him.

Chance ignored him. He wasn't going to get into an argument with the man. Instead he said, "Don't get up. If you do, I'll put you back down again."

"Piss off, ass wipe." James tried to move. Chance grabbed an arm and twisted it. James yelled. He tried to get away, but Chance flipped him over onto his belly and then jabbed a knee into his kidneys.

"Aaaah."

"I *said. Don't. Move.*" Dumb-ass bullies. They always did the opposite of what they were told.

"Chance, they're on their way."

He looked up and spotted Caro standing above them, face pale, eyes wide as she gaped at James.

"Caro," James pleaded. "I just wanted to talk to you."

Chance grunted. "You had your chance when she called you."

"Face-to-face," he added.

"Oh, yeah?" Chance said, leaning in to him. "And shooting her horse was a way to start a conversation."

"I didn't shoot her horse."

"Not with a gun, no, but you shot at her horse with a pellet gun."

James bent back, trying to make eye contact with Caro. "I didn't shoot at you. Honestly."

"Yeah, right," she said.

"What's going on?"

His brother. Word spread fast among the rodeo community when trouble was afoot.

Colt touched Caro's arm briefly. "Did he hurt you?"

"I'm fine," she said, lightly patting his hand. "I didn't let him get close enough to hurt me."

"James!" Colt shouted. "I told you to leave her alone."

"He won't come near her again," Chance said, pressing a little harder on James's wrist. "Right, big boy?"

"Piss off."

"What did he do?" Chance heard someone ask.

"He tried to assault Caro."

"Is this the guy that's been harassing her?"

"He's the one that shot her horse."

"I say we drag him *behind* a horse."

Clearly word had spread about Caro's problem. People were mad. Not surprising. When someone took potshots at livestock, it was kind of a big deal.

"Here, I'll hold him," said one of the wide-shouldered steer wrestlers.

"You can piss off, too," James said.

"Thanks." Chance stood, ignoring the man on the ground and handing over control. The steer wrestler knew exactly where to press, and when Chance was satisfied he had James under control, he sought out Caro. She stared at the man who'd made her life hell. She lifted her head, and their gazes connected. In her eyes, he saw fear, sadness and self-reproach. Before he could think better of it, he crossed to her side and pulled her into his arms.

This.

This was what he'd wanted to do since yesterday. This right here. Hold her. Comfort her. Tell her everything would be all right. She resisted at first, but of course she would. Then she buried her head in his shoulder and it felt good, as if this was where she was supposed to be. Chance met his brother's gaze. Colt was smiling. Or was it smirking? Either way, his small nod seemed to signify approval.

Someone else watched him, too. James.

Yeah, that's right. I'm here to protect her now. Former Army Ranger. Combat ready. And if you touch her again, look out.

The fierceness of his emotions startled him. He'd never felt anything like them in his life. And they were all for Carolina.

SHE COULDN'T GET away from the rodeo grounds fast enough.

Caro tried to let the breeze from the passenger-side window cool her face and her emotions, but it wasn't working.

"They're going to let him go," she said.

"You don't know that," Chance said. "Small-town police departments tend to take a harsher view of people who violate restraining orders, especially when they might have shot a horse twenty-four hours before."

"Yeah, but you know what it's like these days. Nobody ever stays in jail long."

He didn't disagree, and the knot in Caro's stomach

pulled tighter. They were less than a half hour away from home, crossing the San Marcos foothills, the mountains brown from lack of rain, but the scenery no less spectacular. Valley oaks dotted the hillsides, the tips so full of foliage they hung to the ground, providing much-needed shade for wildlife. On any other day, she might have enjoyed the bright blue sky and the fluffy clouds staining the mountains with their shadows. Not today. She had shadows of her own to deal with.

Chanced glanced at her. "When you get back, you should call the officer in charge of your case."

"His name is Officer Connelly, and I already left him a message."

"And I think you need to keep staying at the ranch."

She didn't want to. She wanted life to return to normal. She sighed. "Yeah, I probably should."

That meant more one-on-one time with Chance. A double-edged sword. Last night, she'd woken up from a nightmare only to sense him staring at her. She'd wanted to open her eyes, but she hadn't. If she had, she might have done something stupid like hold out her hand to him. He might have seen what she couldn't hide.

Instead he had slipped away, and she'd tossed and turned, wondering if she should have opened her eyes.

No. She'd done the right thing. She knew that.

Carolina tipped her head back, letting the sunshine soak her face, enjoying the peace it brought her. All too soon, the peace ended when they crossed through the double gates to Reynolds Ranch. She should feel better about coming home—although it wasn't her home. That was the problem. She would be forced to live there for however much longer it would take to get James out of her life.

Chance cleared his throat. "Looks like my sister is here."

She snapped awake. Claire?

Sure enough, Chance's sister stood by the entrance to the barn, one of her rescue dogs sitting at her feet, a smile on her face as they pulled up. Caro couldn't get out of the truck fast enough. She adored Claire Reynolds, soon to be Claire McCall. The woman had been incredibly kind to her the past year.

"I was just leaving you a note," she said, her long black hair so dark and her green eyes so light she always reminded Caro of one of those dolls sold in dime stores with eyes as big as nickels. "Natalie told me you should be home soon."

The front door slammed as Natalie came outside, too. Her baby bump was barely noticeable despite the fact she was due to deliver soon.

"I thought that might be you," she said, her blue eyes echoing the smile on her face. "How was your drive?"

"Long," Carolina muttered before she could stop herself. She cringed. Some of her own self-loathing must have leaked out.

"Colt filled me in," Natalie said kindly. "You going to the police station today?"

She shook her head. "I already called. Officer Connelly isn't on duty today. I have to call first thing in the morning."

"Natalie told me what happened," Claire said, smoothing her black hair, which was clipped up atop her head. The style suited her heart-shaped face. "That's why I brought you Inga." She patted the dog's head.

"Inga?"

Carolina didn't understand. She glanced at Chance

as if he might be in on the secret, but he simply nod-ded knowingly.

Claire's smile was a wide as a sunrise. "I brought you a Belgian Malinois, and she's yours."

"Mine?" Her gaze slipped over them all, settling on Chance.

He had clearly caught on right away, because he said, "She's perfect."

She still didn't get it, not really. "You mean she's mine to keep?"

Claire nodded again.

"You can keep her up in the apartment," Natalie said. "We don't mind. She's house-trained, too. And they're great dogs. I have one, but she's over at Claire's house nursing puppies."

"I don't know what to say."

Claire lifted a hand. "Say yes, but I'll understand if you want to think about it. Trust me, though. Inga needs a job, and you need protecting. It's a match made in heaven."

Inga whined. Caro's gaze fell on the mostly black dog. The animal stared straight at her, bouncing from one paw to another.

"Come on," Claire said, motioning her over. "Make her acquaintance."

Caro walked over slowly, hesitant. "I've never owned a dog before."

"This isn't a dog. This is a military war dog, and they're the closest thing to a human canine you'll ever find. They're a little more high-strung than a normal dog, but with your active life, you won't have any prob-lem with her, and if you do, I'll take her back. Like I said, the main thing is to make sure you're protected."

Caro squatted, showing the dog her hand. Inga immediately licked it. That gave her enough confidence to touch the dog's majestic head. Black eyes that matched her black fur peered back at her. They were specked with brown, just like her coat. She was soft and she smelled like coconut oil. When the dog pushed her head into her, as if to say, "It's okay," a lump formed in her throat.

She looked down at the ground, overwhelmed with gratitude. Her eyes burned, though there was no reason to cry.

No one had ever done anything so nice for her. Everything she'd had, it'd all taken hard work. People didn't give her things, not even temporarily. She sucked in a breath. These people—Claire, Natalie, Colt, Chance—they not only gave from the heart, they cared.

Inga moved. Carolina felt a wet nose against her cheek, then a warm tongue. She closed her eyes, opened her arms and the dog walked into them.

"Thank you," she said, burying her face in the dog's scruff and having to work hard to get the words out over the lump in her throat. "I don't know if I'll be able to keep her. I mean, it would mean moving from my apartment."

"Something you may want to do, anyway," Natalie counseled.

"But I couldn't possibly say no to such an adorable animal." She met Claire's gaze. "This is the kindest thing anyone has ever done for me."

"You're welcome," Claire said with a smile.

"I'll go grab some tea," Natalie said. "We can sit outside and watch you work with her."

When Caro looked up, she spotted Chance gazing down at her, the smile still on his face, his military stance still present despite having been out of the armed services for weeks. She would never forget the way he'd jumped in to help her. The way he'd taken down James. And as he smiled, as he watched her pet her new dog, she admitted how much she liked him and how much she wished he were sticking around. She wanted to be a part of his family. She wanted to know what it was like to have the support of loved ones. To know she would always have a place to come home to.

It broke her heart because she'd never have that.

Chapter Twelve

Chance woke up in the middle of the night, his stomach churning.

The police had released James.

Caro had shared the news yesterday after she'd insisted on going to the police alone. Apparently, it was no big deal when someone violated a restraining order. A felony, yes, but as a police officer had explained to Caro, James wasn't considered armed and dangerous, not without proof. It was his word against hers that he'd shot at her horse, so they'd had to let him go. A slap on the wrist.

Chance hadn't had a solid night's sleep since.

Officer Connelly had tried to reassure her. Told her the police would do what they could. Step up patrols. Yadda, yadda, yadda. Chance knew none of it would work. James was out there. Obsessed. Angry. Insane. Chance had seen it before. He'd probably see it again.

He got out of bed and slipped on clothes without making a noise—he owed this talent to his years in the military. If you disturbed the barrack, something might be thrown at your head. He pulled on his cowboy boots and then headed out into the night.

Carolina's apartment was dark. She was probably

sound asleep, unlike him. Moonlight cast a silvery sheen over the metal roof, the reflection of its face a bright smudge in the middle. It wouldn't be light for hours, but that was okay. His internal clock still wanted him to believe it was midafternoon, Kazakhstan time.

He paused on the front stoop, listening. Nothing but the sound of crickets, and in the far distance, a rooster that appeared to be messed up about the time of day. All was as it should be. Carolina slept, Inga stood guard and the world continued to turn.

It'd been his idea to give her the dog. Claire hadn't balked. She, more than anyone, understood what it was like to be a single woman, alone, with no one to share her life. That would change soon. She would marry Ethan in December. Her Christmas present, she claimed, and Chance couldn't be happier for her.

The barn was dark, too, but he wasn't headed that way. Teddy was kept in a pasture. No fancy stall for him. The old cow horse didn't like being cooped up. It was a simple matter to halter the horse and lead him to the tie rack. Chance didn't know how the animal would take to being ridden, but he needed the practice. Yesterday, while Caro had gone to the police station, he'd pulled one of the Galloping Girlz up behind him from a full-on run. Not once, but several times, and everyone who'd been out there had hooted and hollered. He'd never been so relieved in his life.

"You want to run again?" he asked Teddy, patting the animal on the neck. It'd been years since Chance had taken a midnight ride. Years since he'd knotted the lead rope through the halter and beneath the horse's chin and then swung up without a saddle. When he'd been a kid, riding at night was the only time his dad could be counted on to leave him alone. Zeke had been passed out by then. Too drunk to beat the crap out of him for sneaking a ride on one of his horses. Small miracle Chance and his siblings had turned out normal. He grinned wryly. Well, somewhat normal.

The moon lit the ground a light gray. There was a light over the main barn, which helped to illuminate the outdoor arena. He headed toward it without a second thought, giving old Teddy a warm-up, the midnight air cool against his face. The moisture in the air clung to his face as he broke Teddy into a lope. The horse behaved like the perfect gentleman he was, and that gave Chance time to think.

About *her*.

The look on her face when Claire had given her Inga… It'd been one of such startled gratitude. It was as if no one had ever given her anything before. He realized then he didn't know much about her, and even more startling, that he wanted to know more. Why didn't she talk about her family? What did she like to eat in the morning? Did she prefer ice cream or cupcakes? Country music or pop? *Why?* he asked himself. Why did he want to know? It shouldn't matter. And yet, strangely, it did.

"You going to practice until your legs fall off?"

He damn near fell off Teddy, and it was a sign of how distracted he was that he hadn't seen her approach. *Son of a*— His men would have never let him live such a thing down.

He pulled Teddy up. Carolina peeled herself away from the shadows alongside the barn. That was why he hadn't seen her. She'd purposely stayed hidden.

"I saw you from your window." She pointed over her shoulder at the apartment. Except it wasn't his window. It was only ever supposed to be a temporary stop. Natalie was thinking about hiring an assistant to live there once he was gone and this thing with Caro passed.

"Just thought I'd get in a little more practice."

Her hair caught the moonlight, the blond strands backlit by the light above the barn. She'd left it hanging down, and he wondered if that was because she'd just come from bed. *That* particular thought prompted images he didn't need.

"Wanna try and pull me up?"

Did he want to touch her? No. He had a feeling that a barrier of jeans and a long-sleeved shirt wouldn't be enough to keep him from feeling it again—the sense of possessiveness, the need to protect, the desire to hold her and…do what? Love her and leave her?

"Sure," he answered. Experience had taught him to face his problems, and Carolina had definitely become a problem.

She strolled to the arena gate, slipping through on nearly silent feet, and his heart thumped the way it did the morning of an op. His mouth had gone dry, too. All because of *her*.

"You want to me stand in the middle?" she asked.

On the rail or off to the side, he didn't care. It would all lead to the same thing: touching her. "Wherever you want."

She nodded and stopped in the middle. He took a deep breath, and though he'd practiced the maneuver what felt like a million times, he was nervous. This weekend would be the first time he would need to actually perform Colt's routine, but he'd yet to practice it with Caro. He'd been putting it off.

Teddy seemed to know what they were about to do.

The horse had been through the routine enough times Chance didn't doubt the animal had it memorized. Sure enough, when he lightly tapped the animal on the sides, Teddy lurched into a canter. There was no need to guide him with his makeshift reins. If Chance hadn't been afraid of them slipping over his neck, he would have let them go. Instead he clutched them with one hand, gathering speed as he rounded a corner, the dew so heavy now it stung his face.

Carolina held out a hand. He reached for her, tensing, because things had to be timed perfectly. Teddy would need to slow down and Chance would need to lock his hand with hers. A hand that shook, he admitted, clutching the reins tighter.

Three. Two. One.

They touched. He lost focus, but only for a split second, and then he was pulling and she was swinging and suddenly she was up behind him.

"Good job!"

He'd done it. There would be no need to humiliate himself in front of a huge crowd—

Her hands slipped under his arms, her fingers touching his belly and his stomach contracted from the heat. He tilted left. She corrected right. He clutched Teddy's mane, and somehow they both managed to stay on.

"Sorry," he heard her say, her warm body pressed up against his own. "I didn't mean to startle you."

"You didn't."

It had happened again when they'd touched. Electricity. Fire. Desire.

Son of a—

"Do you want to try it again?"

He grimaced inwardly. "Sure." He pulled Teddy up.

She slipped off and oh, thank God, stopped touching him. It was like stepping from a hot shower and into cool evening air. He could breathe again.

"I'll go to the other side of the arena then."

Teddy knew the drill. There was hardly any need to prompt the horse into a run. The wind felt good against Chance's face. He wished he could still keep running instead of leaning left, holding out a hand then pulling her up behind him.

There it went again.

His pulse. His breathing. His very sanity. The moment she touched him it was all he could do not to lean away from her.

"I think we're good," he said, pulling Teddy up.

"I should probably try to stand."

She smelled like honeysuckle. And that damn fabric softener. "Maybe we should try that when it's daylight."

"Just put him back into a run. It'll take a sec."

If he protested again he'd look like a wimp, and a wimp he definitely was not. So he clucked Teddy forward, the horse completely at ease carrying them around in the dead of night with nothing but bats and owls for an audience. He felt her shirt, the press of her palms against his shoulder. It was a new form of torture, but only because out of nowhere came the image of her touching him elsewhere, and it caused him to stiffen and her to cry out. Before he could help steady her, she'd begun to fall. He couldn't believe it. He'd practiced the move a hundred times with the other girls.

"Caro—"

He was so discombobulated he couldn't quite catch her, and this time she fell on her side, her gasp of pain enough to make him jerk on the rope and stop Teddy.

His heart thundered as he slid off Teddy. "Caro! Are you okay?"

She clutched her ankle. "I'm still sore from falling off the other day."

When James had tried to kill her. Well, maybe not kill her, but certainly ruin her practice session. "Where does it hurt?"

"My ankle."

"Let me see," he said. "Lean back."

"I'll be okay." She tried to push his hands away.

"Just relax. I'm trained for this."

He was also trained to keep his cool while under fire, not fall apart when a woman touched him. He wouldn't dwell on that, though. He needed to remove her boot, a tricky task. He looked into her eyes, and he could tell she tried to hide how much pain she was in.

"Can you take it off?"

He watched her eyes, big and blue, in the moonlight. Her blond hair was mussed, and her lips strained to keep from quivering. He hated seeing her in pain, just as he'd hated seeing the fear in her eyes when James had confronted her.

"I'll be gentle."

He slipped off her boot. She grimaced, but didn't move. He chuckled when he saw her socks. They were black. With smiley faces.

"Happy socks," she explained.

Happy socks. Because she needed something to smile about.

"I like them," he said. "And your ankle doesn't feel swollen."

"I think it's just sprained."

"Let's get you up." He would have to touch her again. "Here." He bent down and slipped an arm behind her.

Shampoo.

He tried not to breathe too deeply as he helped her to her feet. She leaned against him, and his body reacted to how good she felt. It'd been so long...

"I'll help you to your apartment," he said.

"I can walk by myself."

"And hurt your ankle even more? No. I'll wrap it for you once we get to your place. And you should probably stay off it for the rest of the week. Here. Let me turn Teddy loose. Can you stand for a second?"

"Yes."

Sweet relief. That's what he experienced when he stepped away.

Teddy seemed only too happy to be set free in the arena. Chance tossed the halter toward the rail. He'd come back for the horse later. With a deep breath, he headed back to Caro, silently reciting the list of reasons for nipping this damn physical attraction in the bud.

"Ready?" he asked, not wanting to touch her, yet knowing he'd have to slip an arm around her again.

"Ready." She didn't like being a burden. He could see it in her eyes. He spotted something else, too. A shyness that seemed to make it hard for her to look at him. She couldn't hold his gaze for more than a second.

She felt it, too.

It was like discovering the monster under your bed was really a soft, fuzzy toy. A cute little unicorn. Something that could be taken out and played with. He looked away, at the ground.

She wanted him. He wanted her, too.

Life just got a whole helluva lot more complicated.

Chapter Thirteen

He knew.

The thought repeated in her head, the words keeping time with every painful step.

He knew…he knew…he knew.

She'd tried to hide her stupid teenage-like crush from him all week. She knew how dumb it was that she had feelings for him, had been hoping they would fade. And now look at her. Her experiment to prove to herself that touching Chance wouldn't be a problem had completely backfired and nearly broken both of their necks.

Dumb, dumb, dumb.

Those were the next words to keep time with her hops. She felt every hard, sinewy muscle as he helped support her steps. He smelled good. Like talc and pine trees with a hint of cedar.

"Almost there," he said.

Thank God.

They entered the barn, their path barely lit by the light that illuminated the parking area. Horses stirred. Heads popped up. One of them even nickered softly.

"I hope we don't wake up Natalie and Colt."

"We won't," he said, his arm snug around her. "I know for a fact my brother sleeps like the dead."

Why couldn't James have been more like Chance? Chance was the type of man who would do everything in his power to help the weak and infirm. And to protect those he loved. He had integrity, strength and kindness, and she doubted she'd ever meet another man like him.

And he would be gone in a short time.

She knew that. Accepted that. And yet...

Chance paused at the base of the stairway that led to the apartment.

"I can make it from here," she said.

"Up those stairs?" She couldn't see his face all that well, but she could hear the determination in his voice. "Not a chance."

He urged her forward, and together they took the steps one at a time. Caro was relieved once she stood in front of her door. "Okay, thanks. I'm good." She tried to disengage from his arms.

"No. I'm going to take a look at your ankle in the light, get you some ice. Wrap it for you."

Of course he would. He was a man who would take care of a woman, see to her needs. Not abuse her and give her bruises.

When she opened the door, Inga barked. Loudly.

"It's okay, Inga," Carolina said, flipping on the light. Inga wagged her tail, a canine grin on her face. Caro wondered if the dog sensed the kindness of the man at her door.

"Kitchen," Chance said. She hobbled over to the small table and chairs...and it was over. He no longer touched her. She no longer had to smell him and marvel at his strength and otherwise react like a sixteen-year-old girl.

"Ice first," he said. "Set your foot on this chair." He

pulled one out for her, and she did as he suggested. "Let me see."

His fingers brushed her ankle and she gasped, but not because of pain. A bolt of pleasure had zipped through her.

"Sorry," he said.

She slumped in her chair. Her crush on him had gotten *worse*. She couldn't look him in the eyes. With his dark brows and five o'clock shadow, he was too handsome for his own good.

"It doesn't look too bad." He gently turned her ankle. "Definitely swollen, though. You did something to it. Best to stay off it for now."

He carefully set down her foot and headed for the fridge. This was worse. With his back to her, all she could think about was how wide his shoulders were beneath his black shirt. And when he bent to retrieve the tray of ice from the freezer, she noticed how tight his jeans were. By the time he'd finished making her an ice pack, she was as red as the bottle of ketchup in the fridge.

"Here."

"Thanks."

Just leave. She couldn't take humiliating herself anymore. He obviously knew how he affected her, and yet he simply stood over her, staring.

"You going to be okay by yourself?"

No. She didn't want to be alone. She wanted him to be with her, but that was crazy and stupid and ridiculous. Not to mention, never going to happen. Men like him weren't attracted to women like her. They dated smart, beautiful women who ran triathlons and held down six-figure jobs. She was a lowly rodeo trick rider with a messed-up personal life and no family to speak of. Definitely not his type.

"I'll be fine." She forced herself to look into his green eyes. "Thanks."

He frowned, and she wondered if he knew how hard she fought not to grab his hand and pull him down toward her. She tried to hide her thoughts behind an impersonal smile.

"If you need anything," he said, "let me know."

"I will."

He backed away, slowly at first, and then quickly, slipping through the door as if he could read every thought in her mind and as a result couldn't get out of there fast enough. He left her with Inga and her thoughts and a nearly overwhelming ache of pent-up frustration that had her leaning forward and covering her face with her hands.

She moaned.

This sucked.

HE SENT NATALIE to check on her the next day. Why? Because he was a chicken. A big lily-livered, ridiculous chicken who didn't want to face the soft plea in her eyes.

"She's okay," Natalie said, a big smile on her face as she waddled into the kitchen. "A little sore, she said, but she's walking on it this morning. She told me to tell you she'll be good for this weekend's rodeo."

The rodeo.

Never before had he dreaded something as much as he did his solo performance at the Jacksonville rodeo. Another long drive and a longer night spent keeping an eye on Caro.

"You okay?" Natalie asked, settling down behind the

table, no mean feat given her size. Up until a few weeks ago, she'd hid her baby bump well. But she'd suddenly sprouted, the doctor grounding her from all riding activity, which was why she was in the house on a weekday morning, when normally she'd be outside getting the horses ready for a day's worth of riding lessons. His brother and Laney had taken over that task. His sister-in-law was officially on maternity leave.

"I'm fine." He scrubbed a face over his hand. "Long night."

She cocked a bright blond brow, and it occurred to him that she kind of looked like Carolina with her light hair and blue eyes. Carolina was smaller, though, which was good, given her profession.

"Riding at midnight," Natalie huffed. "What were you thinking?"

He was thinking about privacy. About making an ass of himself without anyone watching. About being able to steer clear of Caro, but that hadn't worked out too well.

"It's easier to practice when no one is around."

"You mean when nobody can watch you fall off."

He nodded.

She might have teased him further, but Claire sailed through the front door. She carried a wiggling mass of black fur in her arms. Adam, his sister's son, was right behind her.

"You guys!" Adam yelled. "Youwon'tbelievewhat Ethanwantstodo."

"Adam, slow down," said Claire, smiling at them both. "They can't understand you."

Adam slid to a halt. And Chance nearly laughed as his nephew slowly straightened, took a deep breath, then said slowly, "You won't believe what Ethan wants to do."

"Better," his sister said, her eyes twinkling.

"What does Ethan want to do?" Chance asked.

"Just a second. I need to set this four-legged maniac down on the ground." The tiny Belgian Malinois made a beeline for Natalie.

"Bella!"

Natalie squatted and opened her arms. It wasn't easy for her to bend, but somehow she managed to scoop up the puppy. The excited pup made little snuffling sounds, licking her face and hands and any other available body part.

"I swear that puppy came out of the womb loving you." Claire pulled out a chair next to Chance. "What's up, bro?" she asked, the smile on her face stirring emotions in Chance's heart. He'd never seen her so happy. Not when she'd been married to Marcus, and not before, when she'd been younger. Of course, they'd all had a rough start, but Claire had pulled through. His sister was blissfully in love with Ethan, and it showed.

"Chance is tired," Natalie answered for him. "He was up at midnight practicing the routine."

"Midnight?" Claire said, incredulous.

"Carolina fell off. Hurt her ankle."

"Caro was with you?" Claire asked.

Chance didn't respond. He didn't need to, because he said to Adam, "Go on. Tell me your news. I can tell you're about to burst."

"They were out there together," Natalie said in a stage whisper.

"Ethan wants to start a wounded-warrior therapy program," Adam said, glaring at his aunt, clearly wanting everyone's undivided attention. The look was so much like his sister's, right down to the black hair and green eyes, that Chance almost laughed.

Claire ignored her son. "Chance Reynolds. You could have killed that girl practicing in the dark."

"She's fine." He brushed off her concerns with a wave of his hand. "What do you mean, a wounded-warrior therapy program?"

His sister sat up straighter, and it was clear she didn't want to drop the subject of Carolina, but pride for her husband had won out. She ruffled Adam's full head of hair. A year ago, during his cancer treatment, he'd been as bald as a baby chicken. These days, it was hard to imagine his six-year-old nephew in the battle of his life.

"Ethan wants to open an equine therapy program for veterans," Claire said.

"That's great." Natalie beamed her approval.

"That *is* a great idea," Chance said. He'd heard a lot of positive things about horses and their ability to help PTSD.

"And he said *I* could help," his nephew all but sang, green eyes full of pride.

"Which is a good thing, since we all know how I feel about horses." Claire's eyes were full of amusement.

Yes, he did know. Their dad had ruined riding for Claire, but at least she'd been mounting up more and more lately thanks to Ethan, who loved riding as much as the rest of family.

"I'll make some calls," Chance said. "See if I can't help him out with funding and whatnot."

"That'd be wonderful," Claire said with a wide smile. "If you're not too busy with Carolina, that is."

Claire and Natalie exchanged glances, and Chance

found himself suddenly uncomfortable. So much so he stood to leave.

"Oh, no, you don't." His sister pulled him back down. "We all know you have a thing for her."

He blushed. Actually blushed. "I don't have a thing for Carolina."

"Baloney," Natalie said. She ruffled the fur on her puppy's head, smiling at that animal for a second before pinning Chance with a gaze. "We can see it in your eyes."

"You like Carolina?" said Adam, tipping his head sideways, clearly curious in a you-like-pumpkin-pie kind of way.

"Not like that," Chance lied, and then, as a way of changing the subject, asked, "How's Lady?"

"She's doing great," Claire said. "Gonna wean the puppies next week, including that one." She pointed to Bella. "Now tell us how long you've had a thing for Carolina."

"So you *do* like Carolina?" his nephew asked, clearly confused.

He backed away. "I'm going to go see if Colt needs help saddling up the horses."

"He likes her, all right," Natalie said.

He ignored her, which clearly amused them all, especially when Adam asked, "Do you think he wants to kiss her?" The two of them laughed harder. Damn women.

But as he stepped out on the stoop, he knew he would miss them. He would miss all of this. Miss the mornings when the sun stained the grass the color of lemons. When that same sun lit the tree leaves a bright green. And when the earth smelled of sage, hay and horses. It would be hard to leave.

The realization struck him with the force of a runaway horse.

He'd never wanted to come back to this place. But his brother's insistence had changed his mind. As he looked around him, he understood that his brother had created something from nothing. The only thing recognizable about Reynolds Ranch these days was the old house behind him and the big red hay barn. Everything else—the arena, the new barn, the pastures—it was all different. Better. New.

A home.

He gulped, his stomach churning. Thankfully, the sound of a car coming up the drive distracted him from his thoughts. One of Natalie's clients, no doubt. First lesson of the day. She'd probably wander out soon. Her version of maternity leave was sitting in a lawn chair in the center of the arena schooling her clients. But the car didn't park out in front of the barn. No. It headed straight for the house. Unmarked police car.

His stomach dropped.

He could make out the image of a man inside. He wore a cowboy hat, which made Chance wonder if he were wrong. When the car door popped open and he caught a glimpse of the broad-shouldered man, he knew he'd been right. The man could be a spokesperson for the police officers' association.

"Is Carolina Cruthers here?" he asked. Late thirties. Brown hair and light-colored eyes. He wore a black polo shirt with a gold star on the front, jeans and cowboy boots.

"I'm right here."

They both turned. Caro had appeared at the entrance of the barn, and Chance could tell by the way she played with a strand of her hair that she was nervous. Cops didn't make house calls, not normally, and that this one had could only mean bad news.

Chapter Fourteen

Caro's stomach muscles were stretched so tight someone could strum them like a guitar.

"Sorry," she said, stepping aside to allow Officer Connelly inside her temporary apartment. Chance was right behind him. She'd insisted he join them for whatever news they were about to hear, especially since he'd taken on the task of bodyguard.

"Don't worry about the dog." She motioned for Inga to stay. "She won't hurt you unless I tell her to."

Officer Connelly didn't look convinced as he stared at Inga. Her new dog had the eyes of a predator, and they fixed on the new arrival, gauging whether he was friend or foe.

To give the officer credit, the dog's appearance didn't appear to intimidate the man. "Nice dog."

"Gift from my sister," Chance said. "Former military dog."

"Yeah, I heard there was a rescue out here." The tall man with the dark hair and light eyes looked around. She tried not to let her embarrassment show. She didn't plan on staying long, and so there was still just the couch, the bed, and the rickety old kitchen table and chairs.

"Inga, *sit*," she told the dog when it appeared she

would get up and investigate the new arrival. The dog instantly sat. "Let's go to the kitchen."

The same place she'd sat last night when Chance...

Don't think about that.

"I'm sure you know I've come out here to talk about James." Officer Connelly glanced between the two of them as he took a seat. He was a big man. Taller than Chance, and...thicker. Not fat. Just bigger through the shoulders, arms and legs. Like a prizefighter without the boxing gloves. "Your report to me on Monday made me curious."

Caro's pulse pounded at her neck. She glanced at Chance, who seemed equally on edge.

"Men like your ex don't usually go to such lengths to get back at a woman. I'm not saying it doesn't happen," he said with a quick look at Chance, almost as if he sensed Chance knew differently. "It's just not normal for them to follow someone out of town."

Chance nodded. "That struck me as strange, too."

Caro spread her hands on the table. "Do you believe me now? About him shooting at me?"

Officer Connelly had seemed a bit taken aback she'd reported the incident at the rodeo grounds. It'd almost been as if he'd been defending James, telling her he doubted someone would actually shoot at a horse and that she had to be mistaken. She'd left the police station disillusioned and depressed, especially when she'd learned the other police department had released James once he'd posted bail. But now here was Officer Connelly, and she wondered if she'd had it all wrong. Maybe he'd been playing devil's advocate.

"The fact that Mr. Edwards followed you out of town seemed a little extreme, but I never doubted it was possible. He's clearly stalking you. I started checking around. Went out and spoke to a few people."

He pulled out his cell phone and scrolled until he found what he was looking for. When he did, he read drily, "April, two years ago, charged with assault, never convicted. And a year before that, different town, different assault, but same MO. Charges filed, never convicted. Why?" Officer Connelly stared at the two of them for a long moment. "That's what got me curious. Files said nothing. Just charges dismissed."

"He scares them," Chance speculated.

Officer Connelly's eyes flew up to meet Chance's. He seemed surprised, then impressed. "That's exactly what he does. Terrorizes his victims until they agree to drop the charges."

Caro leaned back in her chair. "But he hasn't made any demands."

"Not yet," Chance said.

Her stomach twisted. This wasn't over, then. Not by a long shot.

"How bad did it get for those other women?"

"Bad enough they refused to testify against him."

James would keep going. Scaring her. Terrorizing her. Driving her crazy.

"What should we do?" Chance asked.

"Be vigilant," Officer Connelly said. "Keep your eyes and ears open."

"That won't be a problem." Chance dropped his words like a grenade—harsh, quick, angry. His face hardened, too. "Son of a bitch will have another think coming if he goes near Caro again."

"Good," Officer Connelly said. "But we have to do things by the book."

"Do we?" Chance lifted a brow, and it was clear by his expression he had his own ideas of how to get James to leave her alone.

Officer Connelly nodded. "He needs to be put away. Legally. With a public record."

Chance leaned forward. "My way won't clog up the judiciary system."

What Chance talked about was wrong, but it still made her feel protected, safe and, yes, relieved he would go to such lengths.

She touched his arm briefly. "Chance, it's okay. We'll figure out a way to lock him behind bars."

Connelly's eyes had never left Chance's. "Caro tells me you're ex-military."

"Army Ranger."

"Shame to mess up a future career in law enforcement out of a need for revenge."

"Who said I was going into law enforcement?"

She watched as Officer Connelly sized Chance up. He frowned, apparently disappointed by what he saw. "Private contracting then?"

Chance nodded. "When the time comes."

Another long stare. "There are other ways to serve your country, you know."

Caro didn't understand what was going on between the two of them. Chance suddenly gripped the edge of the table, appearing capable of injecting venom into someone's veins. She leaned forward to get their attention. "Can we get back on topic?"

Chance had the grace to look abashed. Officer Connelly seemed amused, but he shot her a look of apology.

"Did you confront James about what happened at

the rodeo grounds?" she asked. "His shooting at me, I mean."

"He denied it. No surprise." Officer Connelly shook his head. "But reading his files, I have no doubt he's capable of doing that and much more."

"Maybe you should stay home this weekend," Chance said.

"No." She looked between the two men. "I won't let him ruin my life. Trick riding is my job. I get paid to do it. No work, no money and I'm broke enough as it is."

She hated admitting that in front of Chance. She already felt like a failure, but she needed him to understand he couldn't ground her. She had to work, especially if she wanted to switch apartments. She'd need a security deposit, and she had Inga to take care of now. She glanced at the dog.

"She goes where you go," Chance said, clearly following her gaze. "Even to the rodeos."

"Good idea," Officer Connelly said.

Chance shot him a look that obviously indicated he didn't need his approval, and then he shifted his attention back to her. "This weekend, you'll stay in the trailer with me again. I'll tell the girls they should stay with friends. It occurred to me last weekend he might think you're in there with them and do something aimed at hurting you, but injuring all of them instead."

She hadn't thought of that, and the idea sickened her. She'd never forgive herself if someone got hurt because of her poor choice of a boyfriend.

"Let me know if anything else happens." Officer Connelly stood. "I've put my cell phone on my card. Call me, even if it's on a weekend." He slid the card across the table. She caught his full name then. Brennan Connelly.

"Thank you," she said.

Officer Connelly turned when he reached the door. "I know it might be tough, but don't let James bully you. That's what he's used to doing—and getting away with it. I would hate to see that happen again."

She nodded. "I don't plan on letting him get close to me."

"Good."

The moment the door closed behind the officer, Chance said, "I still think you should stay home this weekend."

"No."

"If it's money you need, I'm sure Colt could put you to work around the ranch, especially with Natalie out of commission."

"No," she said more firmly, meeting his gaze, though doing so caused her stomach to flip. "I'm going to keep on doing what I do no matter what James throws in my direction."

She thought he might argue the point, but instead he smiled—a small one, but it was enough to make her look away, her cheeks filling with color.

"He's not going to hurt you."

She nodded, still refusing to look at him.

"I won't let him."

It was torture, him sitting across from her. Caro was aware of his smell and his heat, and, yes, damn it all, the primordial desire to be with him. He was a man who would do anything to protect her from harm. That was the attraction. It was stupid and cave woman–ish, but she couldn't help herself.

"Caro?"

Could he see her breath quickening? Did he spot the pulse at the base of her neck? Had he taken note of how she clenched her hands into fists?

"I should call the other girls." She stood, too quickly, and pain shot up her leg. She tilted to the left.

And he caught her.

The world turned topsy-turvy. Her whole body ignited. Her gasp wasn't because her ankle hurt. It was because her body lit up like she had fireworks inside of her, all booms and wooshes and zaps, and now she tingled in places she didn't want to think about.

"Sorry," she said, her face heating. "I forgot about my ankle."

He seemed puzzled by her reaction. Or maybe it was concern she read in his eyes. And surprise. "You shouldn't be walking on it."

"I'm fine." She hopped for the couch, where she'd left her phone, and though she tried to hide it, she would bet he could see her grimacing. "I'll see you later on for practice."

"No," he said sharply. "You need to stay off that ankle for at least a couple days."

They needed to practice, to nail down the fine points of their new routine, yet she couldn't find the courage to argue the point.

"Yeah, maybe you're right."

His eyes lit up. With relief?

"I'll send Natalie up here to check on you later."

"Thanks."

And he was gone. She grabbed one of the couch pillows, covered her face with it and screamed.

Chapter Fifteen

The Jacksonville rodeo grounds were nestled in the Diablo mountain range, halfway between the Bay Area and the Central Valley. It was pretty country, Chance thought. Different from the Sierra foothills, with more oaks and fewer pine trees. Warmer, too.

Caro had caught a ride to the rodeo grounds with one of the girls. He shouldn't have felt grateful that she wanted to ride with her friends. He should have insisted she go with him, but he didn't. When she'd collapsed against him the night before, he'd nearly gasped from the reaction her touch had ignited. The thought of sitting next to her for the six-hour drive to the Jacksonville rodeo grounds was unbearable.

"So you're flying solo this weekend, huh?"

Chance turned to see who'd spoken, smiling when he caught sight of Bill walking toward him. They'd been reintroduced at the last rodeo, but it was as if Chance had never stopped competing on the high school rodeo circuit where they'd both started out. Bill was still the wisecracking funny man he'd always been.

"Yup. Gonna be performing on my own. Hope I don't run you down."

"Nah," the little man said, shaking his hand. Tonight

his face would be covered with black makeup and the cowboy hat he currently wore would be replaced with a backward baseball cap. He'd be wearing clothes three times too big, too. Bill was one of the best barrel men in the industry, someone who wasn't afraid to throw himself in front of a fifteen-hundred-pound animal and who would do whatever it took to keep someone safe. Chance respected that more than Bill probably knew.

"Cutting things kind of close, aren't you?" he said with a wide smile. "Rodeo starts in a couple hours."

"We decided to leave this morning." He frowned. "For security reasons."

Bill's face darkened. "You really think that guy will come after Caro again?"

"*That guy* needs his ass kicked," Chance muttered. "He sent her a text this week." Just thinking about it sent his blood pressure soaring. "Told her he couldn't wait to see her perform this weekend."

Bill stroked his face. "Hasn't she got a restraining order against him or something?"

"Restraining orders only do so much." Chance tipped his cowboy hat back. "So, yes, we think there's a good chance he'll be here. It's a public event, and as long as he stays at least a thousand feet away, technically, he can do whatever he wants." He looked around, taking in the barren hills, the flat terrain and the aluminum grandstands that seemed to jut up out of nowhere. An elementary school sat in the distance, and beyond that, the only residential area of town. Jacksonville was truly a single-stoplight town with one grocery store, a tiny strip mall and not much else. "At least we should be able to see him coming."

"And everyone knows what he looks like," Bill said with a nod.

Chance had asked Caro for a picture of James. They'd distributed it to every person they could think of via social media, asking everyone to share. They hoped it would keep people on the alert.

"Extra eyes on the ground should help," he said, turning back to the trailer. "My plan is to set up a corral by our rig. The other girls are going to stay with friends. Caro's staying with me. That's why I pulled in next to you. I was hoping I could use one side of your trailer as a wall. I can make a bigger corral that way."

"Sure," Bill said.

They set to work, but it didn't take them long to erect the portable panels Chance had brought. Having to use only three sides helped. He'd be able to pull the work trailer in and out when he performed. Caro and the other girls arrived shortly thereafter, and Chance did his best to ignore her while keeping an eye out for James. They filled hay bags and water buckets. Finally, they unloaded the horses.

"Guess we should probably get ready," Caro said, gazing up at him with trepidation in her eyes. It killed him every time. He hated seeing her worried. Hated that some lowlife putz of a man could wreak such havoc with her nerves. She had enough on her plate as it was.

"Don't think about it," he said. "He sent you that text to mess with your mind, that's all. I doubt he'll be here this weekend."

She tried to put on a brave face, and damn it, he admired her for it. "I'm going to head over to Lori's trailer and get ready."

He needed to get ready, too. The trailer was part of the act, which meant he'd need to pull it closer to the arena.

His first solo performance.

Okay, yes, that had him a little on edge, too. He'd been practicing for weeks, all of it leading up to this moment, and as his brother had said, there was no dress rehearsal in this business. You had to dive in and do it, and while Chance hadn't fallen off the horse once this week, there was always the possibility something could go wrong during a live performance.

It didn't take him long to dress, and he wouldn't need to move the trailer until it was time for his act, but that didn't stop his hands from shaking as if he was back on the front lines. He tried to keep himself busy, checking in with the rodeo manager, making sure the pen they'd erected wouldn't fall down, double- and even triple-checking buckets and feed bags. When Chance heard the first roar of the crowd, he nearly jumped, which irritated him to the point he almost bit the head off a little girl who stuck her hand between the metal rails to pet Rio. Her look of terror and distress made him realize he needed to calm down. He wasn't facing a firing squad. Compared to running for his life, this was small potatoes.

From that point forward, he kept himself firmly in hand. They were surrounded by trailers, with cowboys and cowgirls riding by. Chance scanned each person. Ever vigilant. Always on the alert.

"You ready?"

He turned to see Caro standing behind him, looking as sexy as ever in her stop sign–red trick-riding outfit. She'd pulled her long blond hair into a ponytail and applied extra makeup Not that she needed it. Her blue eyes always looked bright, but with eyeliner and mascara, they glowed like the stars in the sky. A ridiculously poetic thing to think, but it was true.

"As ready as I'll ever be."

She smiled. "See you over there."

He watched her grab Rio from the pen. She'd already saddled him earlier, so it was a simple thing to slip on his bridle. She mounted up shortly after, beautiful, confident and completely at ease. It made him feel like an idiot for being nervous.

You've faced men with rifles pointed at your head. This is just a little rodeo. And a small-town one at that.

It didn't feel small-town.

Concentrate on the routine.

He did a mental run-through: Teddy in the trailer. Pull into the arena. Let Teddy out. First trick is circle Teddy. Right circle. Left circle. Stop. Rear. Dance on hind legs. Dance on all four legs. Stop. Teddy bares his teeth and smiles at the crowd. Bow. Climb aboard. Stand again. Circle without reins and wave. The girls come in then. They perform. Bill jumps at Caro. He rescues Caro. Caro ropes Bill. Done.

Simple.

With a deep breath and a calm resolve, he untied Teddy and loaded him up. He checked his reflection in the driver-side window to make sure his black cowboy hat wasn't crooked and then climbed into the truck and started the engine.

Ready or not, here I come.

It took a bit to make his way to the arena, but once he was close, rodeo officials cleared a path. He hung back from the rear gate, watching as the last of the saddle bronc riders tried to cover their mounts, all the while keeping an eye on the grandstands, the people milling around, even the people on horseback. This rodeo was a security nightmare, but he had no choice except to roll with it.

His teammates arrived. They lined up next to Caro and Rio outside the arena. Over the previous month, he'd learned their names: Judy, Lori, Ann, Delilah. All of them young, lithe and amazing, but none of them as pretty as Caro. He spotted more than one cowboy eyeing the pretty blonde as she sat atop her horse, waiting. With her hair pulled back and her regal posture, she looked like a vision an artist would sculpt.

Someone tapped his window.

"You ready?" asked one of the rodeo producers.

He gave the thumbs-up.

Through the exterior of the truck, he heard the words, "Ladies and gentlemen, we've got a special treat for you this weekend."

The surge of adrenaline shooting through him made it hard to breathe. He told himself to relax as someone opened the gate, but he still needed to clutch the steering wheel to steady his hands. The truck's engine strained once the tires sank into the deeper footing. Chance tried to ignore the hundreds of faces staring down at him. His hands gripped the wheel so tight his knuckles started to hurt.

"The Jacksonville rodeo welcomes Chance Reynolds and his amazing rodeo misfit, Teddy!"

That was his cue. He slipped out of the truck and the roar of the crowd nearly made him stumble backward. He could feel their presence, like an invisible force field that touched him and stirred something inside him. He waved as he headed for the back of the trailer.

"Ladies and gentlemen, Chance Reynolds comes from a long line of rodeo performers. The horse he's performing with today is a second-generation trick horse, and you won't believe what he can do."

Looking into the horse's soulful eyes helped calm his nerves. Teddy had done this act hundreds of times. He'd probably do all the moves without commands, so it was simple for Chance to step back and let the horse out. The crowd cheered when Teddy paused and nodded his head, his long mane flying, one of his front legs pawing the ground. Colt said that happened sometimes, that Teddy loved to perform, and he would ham it up in front of certain crowds. Clearly, today was one of those days.

"Okay, kid, let's do it."

He motioned for the horse to circle. It was like being at home. Teddy set off with a flick of his head, and when he finished one circle, he changed directions. The crowd roared its approval. Chance gave the command to stop. The audience seemed to hold its breath. Chance lifted his arm. Teddy reared. There were gasps and cries of delight and then more applause, the cheers growing louder as Teddy began to hop, or dance, one hop, two, three. Chance began to relax. It was so easy, his brother's constant schooling coming to his aid. He didn't need to think about the next move. He simply gave the signal for Teddy to stop, and then without him asking, the horse pranced in place. Beautiful to watch. Perfect performance.

Chance blinked. Out of nowhere, he thought of another black horse, a beautiful black mare that his dad had beaten into submission. The image made him wince. She'd been a heck of a performer, too, but Teddy performed out of love, not fear. His brother had done a remarkable job with the rescue, using a kind touch and a gentle heart. And it showed. The horse seemed to read Chance's thoughts, smiling at the crowd all on his own.

"Teddy, bow," he told the horse, and the animal stretched his front legs apart, his head sinking between his knees.

"How about that, ladies and gentlemen? But it's not over yet. Welcome to the Jacksonville rodeo arena the Galloping Girlz!"

And that was Chance's cue to hop aboard. Trick riders used a line of people holding paper streamers to keep their horses from ducking off the rail. He would join those people, albeit aboard Teddy, and hold out his hand so the girls could slap it on their way by. Carolina circled around behind him, and Chance turned just in time to see Bill the Barrel Man jump out of his can. Chance laughed. Bill wore a black scarf over the bottom half of his face and a hat big enough to cover the state of Wyoming.

"How in the hell…" He had no idea how he'd fit the damn hat into the barrel.

"Here goes," Chance whispered to himself.

He'd never practiced the routine with Bill, but no one would have known it. It went exactly as it had the previous weekend when Colt had played the part of hero. Caro was perfect, too, screaming when Bill seemed to snatch her off her horse. And sore ankle or not, she landed perfectly. Bill wagged his eyebrows at the crowd, and the audience laughed, booed and happily played along.

It was time.

Chance nudged Teddy forward in Caro and Bill's direction. The horse needed next to no instruction. Caro threw her hand out. Chance leaned down, reached for her, and she flung herself up behind him. Somehow it all worked. Just as they'd practiced.

The crowd thundered their approval.

Chance was acutely aware of Caro's presence, but it was okay this time. He didn't falter. Didn't mess it all up like he had so many times before. Today they were on fire. A team. And it felt...perfect.

They galloped toward the truck and trailer. Caro reached for the rope. She scooped it up smoothly and then stood. This, too, the audience loved, because they'd figured out what she meant to do. Bill made a big production of trying to run away, big hat flopping, pants slipping down, and suddenly Chance wanted to laugh, too. He'd never felt so free before. So at home. So perfectly at ease.

Caro's rope slid around Bill's waist, and the barrel man's arms became pinned to his side. The audience laughed, hooted and cheered. Caro somehow managed to tug Bill off his feet while standing up on Teddy and holding on to Chance. That wasn't supposed to happen. Bill was supposed to fight the rope on his feet, but the barrel man rolled with it. The coup de grâce came as they dragged Bill out the arena. The man had layered his clothes, and they began to slide off him. Bill left behind first his black pants and then what looked like a pair of sweats and then another layer of...something. Boxer shorts, maybe. Chance struggled to keep a straight face as Caro jumped down, and he turned Teddy back toward the arena.

"Ladies and gentlemen, give a hand for Chance Reynolds, will you? And the Galloping Girlz and the wonder horse Teddy!"

The roar of the crowd was something to behold, and

as Chance stood in the middle of the arena, waving, smiling and drinking in their applause, he realized he could get used to this. His gaze snagged on Caro standing outside the arena. Even from a distance, he could see the glint of her blue eyes. She grinned at him, and he couldn't help but grin back.

He could get used to a lot of things if he weren't careful.

Chapter Sixteen

He seemed distracted, Caro thought, as they sat outside the trailer later that night. It was so unlike Chance that Caro wondered if there was something wrong.

"Were you unhappy with our performance?" she asked.

His green eyes shot to hers, and his handsome face flinched.

"God, no."

And that was all he said. Two words. She supposed she should be grateful for that.

They'd stowed all the horse tack away in silence. Of course, her teammates had been around then and she hadn't been put off by his lack of talking. But then the girls had left—gone to a rodeo dance or something. Caro had changed into a gray T-shirt and jeans and joined Chance outside. Still nothing. They sat beneath the trailer's awning, watching the horses eat their dinner in the makeshift corral. The sun set slowly behind them.

"You're so quiet," she ventured to say.

"Just tired." He took a sip of his beer.

Maybe she should have gone with the girls. However, fending off the advances of drunken cowboys had never been her thing. And with the threat of James looming, she would have been a fool to step out of Chance's protective custody.

She grimaced. It would probably beat sitting next to him in silence, wondering what it would be like to be with him, to be his in every sense of the word.

"I'm going inside," she said.

Ridiculous. It wasn't dark yet—not all the way. Dusk had dimmed the lights, but she could still see his face beneath his cowboy hat. He acknowledged her words with a tip of his beer bottle.

That hurt.

She had no idea why. She didn't want him to fawn all over her. She was too independent for that. A little conversation would be nice, though. So it would be far easier to be out of sight, where he'd be out of mind, and she would stop thinking about what might have happened if she'd met Chance before James. Things might have been different. She might not have felt so nervous, on edge and confused when he was near. Handsome cowboys had always been a weakness, but they were usually more trouble than they were worth and that was a lesson she should have learned by now.

"'Night." She started to turn away, but then quickly added, "Thanks for dinner."

"Welcome."

And that was that.

"Crap," she muttered, slipping inside the trailer. "Crap, crap, crap, crap."

She missed Inga. Maybe she should have brought the dog like Chance had said, but the thought of leaving her locked up in the trailer all day didn't seem right, not yet, at least. Not until she learned what it meant to travel. And so she'd left her behind. Now she wished she could hold her tight. Dogs loved people no matter how undeserving they were.

At least you're not afraid of Chance anymore.

She almost laughed. That was an understatement. Working together had changed that. Actually, last weekend, when he'd jumped to her defense, had changed that. The man would never hurt her. He would die trying to protect her. Actually *die*. *Some* men were worthy of love. James wasn't.

She sat down on the couch, and just like she had back at home, picked up a pillow and covered her face with it, screaming. She wanted to let loose some more. To deafen her own ears with her frustration, but she couldn't, not if she didn't want Chance charging in, coming to her rescue.

"What's wrong?"

She damn near dropped the pillow.

Chance.

"I heard you scream."

"I, uh." What to say? "Stubbed my toe."

Lame.

"You stubbed your toe?" he repeated, glancing at her boot-clad feet.

He had to know she was lying. She'd never been very good at it.

"It was the bad leg. Jarred my ankle."

His gaze narrowed. "Let me have a look."

"No, no." Because there he went again. Sir Galahad. The man could make her feel like a princess in need of rescuing. "I'm all right."

Except her nipples were erect.

She caught a glimpse of them as she glanced down

at her foot. She planted the pillow over her midsection so fast he glanced at her askance.

She could see the spark in his eyes. He knew she felt the current of electricity between them. That she'd had fantasies about him. That when they'd performed together it was all she could do not to kiss him after his so-called rescue.

He knew.

"I think maybe I should leave," she said softly. She meant sleep somewhere else. Somewhere far from her thoughts and desires.

"Maybe you should."

It was all the proof she needed to know she'd read him correctly. She stood, her humiliation so acute her cheeks burned with a nearly physical pain. He must think her one of those women, the kind that couldn't keep her hands off men and went from one man to the next. She wasn't that type at all. She'd spent weeks warning herself away from him, and look where it'd gotten her—more attracted to him than ever before.

"I'm sorry."

She tried to rush past him, but he stepped in front of her. "Don't."

She didn't want to look at him. She really didn't. "Don't what?"

He inhaled deeply before he said, "Don't leave. It's not safe out there."

And it was then, at that precise moment, that Caro realized he fought it, too. That everything she felt, he did, too. That the desire coiling in her belly, teasing and taunting her, also teased and taunted him. Made his hands shake like hers. For some crazy, insane reason the realization made her want to cry.

Lord help her. Lord help them both.

"Maybe I could sleep with the girls—"

"No," he said sharply. He lifted his hands, gently touched her cheeks. "Stop saying that." He peered intently at her with eyes the color of jade. "You can stay right here, where you'll be safe."

Her eyes filled with tears. She had never felt so cherished and cared for in her life. "Thank you," she said softly. But now it was time to be brave. To be bold and do something she would never have done before James.

She stood on tiptoes and lightly kissed him.

He froze. She didn't move, either, just stared into his kind green eyes. And then she did another brave thing. She walked away. Outside. Into the cold night air. Where they wouldn't be tempted to do something crazy.

And that was the point.

SHE LEFT HIM standing there, and Chance wanted to follow. Lord, how he wanted to grab her hand, to jerk her to him. Instead he went to the fridge and grabbed another beer.

What the hell?

He removed his cowboy hat and tossed it onto the couch. He swiped a hand through his hair. What the hell was he thinking? She wasn't the one who should be leaving. He was.

"Caro, wait."

He flung open the trailer door. She sat outside, and his relief she hadn't gone far made him clutch the door handle tighter. That's what happened when you became distracted. When you lost your focus. You lost sight of the objective. Keeping her safe was the objective.

"Come inside." He took a deep breath, trying not to

focus on how pretty she looked sitting in the half-light of dusk. His lips tingled where hers had brushed his own.

She looked up at him, and the gratitude in her eyes caused him to feel things he probably shouldn't.

"I'll sit outside and keep watch."

"Like you did last weekend?"

Did she know he'd spent the whole night outside? True, she'd found him in the morning, but she couldn't know he'd been out there all night.

She knew.

"You don't have to do that," she said, clasping her hands in her lap. "James wouldn't dare come after me with you around, not after what happened last time."

No. He wouldn't. "Things are just easier if you come inside."

She sighed and gazed at the horses. Her blond hair caught the fiery dusk light.

"What a pair we are," she said. "Two grown adults. One of us who seems to be genetically programmed to pick the wrong man. Another one of us with a long history of keeping himself unattached, or so I've heard."

Her words drew him out of the trailer. What was the point of trying to fight it anymore?

"I stay out of relationships for a reason," he said.

She held out her hand. It took him a moment to realize she wanted a sip of his beer, a beer he'd forgotten he was holding. Watching her take a sip, seeing the way her lips wrapped around the opening of the bottle... Well, he needed to look away.

"I know," she said. "Your sister told me."

"Oh, yeah? What else did she tell you?" he asked, sitting next to her. This was a mistake. He should have stayed in the trailer. Or one of them should have.

"That you never let yourself get too close. You keep your distance as a way of protecting yourself. You stayed away all these years because you can't face the truth."

"And what truth is that?"

She pinned him with a stare. "That you're afraid." She took another sip of his beer. "All the places you've been. All the gunfire you've faced, but the thing you most fear? Caring about something too much."

"What?"

She nodded. "That's what Claire said."

"She's wrong."

She handed his beer back to him and shrugged. "Maybe."

He stared at the opening of the bottle. He wasn't afraid of caring. He loved his family so much he fought for their freedom.

"But you know what I just realized?" She met his gaze again. "So what? You're a damn fine man, Chance Reynolds. Any girl would be lucky to spend just one night with you."

"Excuse me?"

"I don't need commitment, or want it," she said, leaning toward him. "I just want one night. And before you say it, I know you plan to leave soon and never come back. I understand."

What was she saying?

"I'm going back inside the trailer." She stood slowly. "I'll be waiting there for you. If you don't follow, that's okay. But if you do, I think it'll be a night neither of us will ever forget."

She walked by, touching him on her way past, just a brief caress, but enough to convince him she was right.

Something awaited him. Something that might be remarkable and spectacular. Something he should maybe avoid at all cost.

Something he was helpless to resist.

Chapter Seventeen

Would he follow?

Lord, Carolina didn't know.

All she knew was she had to try. What if he was the man of her dreams? What if tonight was her one chance to hold him? What if she could convince him to stay?

She knew it likely wouldn't happen. Men like him didn't give up entire careers for women like her. But what if there was a chance he might?

He wasn't coming.

She stood in the middle of the trailer, waiting, her pulse speeding up with each passing second. If she couldn't convince him to stay, so what? Chance was the most virile, attractive, sexy man she'd ever met. Unbelievably good-looking and thoroughly masculine. Was it wrong of her to want to spend a night with him? What red-blooded female wouldn't want that?

The trailer door opened.

She couldn't breathe. Her heart seemed to stop beating because the look in his eyes…

The air gushed from her lungs. Her knees grew weak, *literally* weak. She swooned like a heroine in an old Western movie. "You can't tell my family about this," he said, his voice rough. "My brother would never approve."

"No," she said, her skin tingling and igniting like a live wire because there it was again—a surge that hit her whenever he was near. A singe of heat seemed to sear her to the soul, telling her he would do things to her no man had ever had done before.

"And it'll only be this one time."

"I know."

Just quit talking.

"Caro—"

She made the decision for him, going to him, brushing her body up against his, nearly gasping at how good it felt to finally drop the barriers and set the attraction free.

His eyes flared. She waited, hoping he would reciprocate. His head slowly lowered to her own.

Bliss.

The touch of his lips was like trick riding in front of an audience. Addictive. Electrifying. Crazy.

Yes.

The word sang through her brain as she tipped her head sideways and opened her mouth. *Yes*, she thought again, feeling his tongue slip between her lips and caress her own. *Yes*, she sang as he swirled his tongue around her own, stroking her, teasing her, taunting her.

She pressed her hand against his chest. He was so physically fit. It turned her on. Everything about the man aroused her. She wanted to be with him. To touch him. To please him in a way he'd never been pleased before.

"Chance," she murmured, pressing herself against him, sliding up the length of him.

"Jesus."

It was all he said, but it was enough. She grew bold, touching him there, feeling his pulse beneath her fingers as his whole body stilled. Everything inside her reveled at the fact she'd done that. She'd made him react.

He pushed her up against the trailer wall. It should have scared her. It should have reminded her of James. But it didn't. It turned her on because she wanted him against her.

"What are you doing to me?" he mumbled.

He lifted her up. She wrapped her legs around his waist, the center of him against her own core. Her whole body contracted and pulsed in response. He kissed her again, hard, and he was so strong he could have easily used brute force, but he didn't. She loved that about him.

She lifted her hips. He grunted, kissed her harder, and she knew that all he need do was continue holding her like he was and she would lose it. She would shatter into a million pieces. And only his arms would hold her together.

Chance's hand slid up her side toward her breast, and she almost shattered right then because the feel of him cupping her, squeezing her, melding her...

She drew back, gasped, "Bed."

His eyes were a smoky black. "Yeah," he said. "Bed."

JUST ONE NIGHT.

The words repeated in Chance's head as he carried Carolina toward the trailer's bedroom.

God, he wouldn't last, not if she kept kissing him like she did. And touching him and moving against him. Almost in self-defense he tossed her onto the bed, but if her body had set him on fire, the look in her eyes nearly drove him to the edge.

Her hands tugged at the edge of her shirt, lifting it,

teasing him with a glimpse of her flesh first, then all of it.

He simply stood, watching.

A part of him marveled, took a snapshot of the moment, fixing in his mind how she looked: tousled hair, glittering eyes, pouty mouth. She could have tempted a holy man to give up his vows, and he was no holy man.

Chance didn't want to move. He feared spooking her and inadvertently stopping her sexy striptease. She took the choice away from him, shooting forward, her gaze scanning him, her hand slowly reaching for him. Her palm landed on his chest, and he closed his eyes. Her hand slipped lower, and he knew what she would do. Still, he gasped when she touched him. She tipped her head sideways, pressed up against him, her tongue hot and warm slipping between his lips. Dear Lord. Sweet... so sweet. Like molasses and brown sugar and hot sauce. He couldn't get enough of her.

He slipped a palm beneath her bra. He felt bare flesh and heat, and he suddenly wanted more. He leaned her back against the bed and slid his lips against her bare flesh.

"Chance," she said softly, his name both a groan and a verbal caress. Her hips lifted upward.

His hands found the waistband of her jeans, and he popped the button, slid the zipper free. He tugged them down, and the sight of her tiny pink underwear shot a fresh spurt of heat through him. They matched her bra, which her breasts spilled out of, nipples still hard.

"You're going to be the death of me," he groaned.

"What a sweet death," she answered with a crooked smile.

Something inside him flipped. He pulled her boots

and her jeans off in one motion and then simply gazed. She had the body of an athlete and the beauty of a swan. He couldn't wait to taste her. All of her.

His head lowered. She arched upward again. His mouth found her thighs. His hands found her center, and she let out a groan that drove him almost over the edge. He tasted the salty sweetness of her flesh. He held her down because she writhed beneath him. The ache in his groin turned into a burn.

"Chance," she said, sitting up, her hands finding his. She pulled him up and he couldn't resist.

Their lips found each other's again, but this time her hands were between them. She unbuckled his belt and then unbuttoned his pants. She slid his boxers down. He kicked off his boots, and a second later, his jeans and everything else. He was right where he wanted to be. With Caro. He opened his eyes and gazed into twin blue pools. He slid his fingers into the thick depths of hair, testing its weight and its silkiness.

"Are you sure?" he asked.

She nodded. "I've never been more certain of anything in my life."

Her eyes sparkled like stars. She slowly unbuttoned his shirt and slipped it down his shoulders. Her heat called to him, filling him with a feeling he didn't know. It made him feel awkward, clumsy and inept. She challenged him to be his best, and he worried he would disappoint. "My turn," she said, slipping her bra straps down one at a time.

He helped her slide the garment off. She was the prettiest thing he'd ever seen with her hair fanned out beneath her. She never took her eyes off him, and he didn't want her to. It made their act all the more erotic to have her begging him with her eyes.

What are you doing to me? he silently asked.

Almost as if she heard the question, she lifted a hand and touched the side of his face. His nipples grazed her chest and she gasped. He lowered his head, his lips finding her hardened nubs. Her hips thrust upward and it was almost his undoing, but somehow he held on to control as he nipped and suckled her. She groaned in pleasure.

She pulled him up. He knew what she wanted. He wanted it, too, anticipating their kiss as he'd never anticipated anything before. Her lips were like butterfly wings. He nuzzled them apart, and when they kissed once more, he knew he'd never taste anything so perfect again. He gently nudged her legs apart. She opened for him, welcoming his length. Chance closed his eyes because slipping into her was like coming home.

She wrapped her legs around him. Hard. She moved her hips. Fast. She clutched him to her. Tight.

Lord…

He wouldn't last. She moved beneath him as though she knew his every desire. He lost all sense of time, space and himself. They were joined not just physically, but emotionally, mentally and through a tenuous connection he couldn't quite explain.

"Chance."

He heard the same need for release he felt, and so he kept the rhythm going faster and faster and faster until her cry echoed his own. He spiraled down a well of pleasure he'd never experienced before.

His breaths matched hers.

That was his first coherent thought, which was amazing given she held him so tightly it was a wonder he could breathe. Slowly, her hold loosened until he was able to shift back and look into her eyes.

She smiled.

He couldn't breathe. It was the smile of an angel, and it called to his heart.

Chance knew nothing would ever be the same again.

CAROLINA AWOKE WITH sadness clinging to her heart.

For a long moment, she simply lay in his arms, absorbing the heat of his body, listening to the steady drone of his pulse, admiring the taut smoothness of his skin. The sun had just started to rise. It cast a pale glow over them both.

Sad.

She'd known it was only for a night. She'd gone into this with her eyes wide-open. But as he'd held her, as he'd brought her to pleasure over and over again last night, each time had been a little more bittersweet, a little more heartbreaking.

"What are you thinking about?"

His words startled her. She looked up and realized his gaze was upon her. She lifted up on her elbows.

"Long day," she improvised. "We won't get home until midnight."

His hands found her shoulders, his thumb brushing her bare skin in a comforting way. "We could always stay another night."

Everything inside her stilled.

"I could call Colt and tell him the truck won't start. We could hang out here until morning."

But as quickly as the rush of pleasure warmed her, it faded, leaving coldness in its wake. And then what? Delay the inevitable? She almost said those exact words, but she didn't want him to know how much his suggestion tempted her. She'd made it clear last night that she understood their being together was a onetime thing. He needed to know she meant it.

"Nah," she said as dismissively as possible. "We should probably get back."

He would never know how hard it was for her to pull away from him, to get dressed as if nothing out of the ordinary had happened, to slip on her clothes. Or how difficult she found it not to race back and kiss him once she was done. But she knew this man. She knew if she pushed him and gushed over him, he would run. She didn't know how she knew that. She just did. So Carolina kept her cool as she headed out the front door, pausing and giving him what she hoped was an impersonal wave goodbye.

He never saw her collapse against the door. Never saw her close her eyes, nor the way her lips silently formed the word *damn*.

Chapter Eighteen

She was true to her word.

Chance didn't know what to think. Carolina had ignored him for the rest of the day, simply going about her business and acting as if nothing had happened between them, and that left him...

He tried to think of the word.

Confused.

When they performed later that afternoon, she did not give away their intimacy. She treated him like a prop—which he supposed, in a way, he was—completing her portion of the act and then dashing out afterward. By the time he drove back to their spot, she was already waving goodbye.

"Gonna catch a ride back with the girls," she said, barely giving him a smile before ducking her head into the truck and taking off.

He almost called after her, wanting to tell her it was a bad idea, that she should stay with him and help him load up the panels because they never knew if James was around, but that was an excuse and she would know it. She'd be fine on the road with the girls. He'd made sure each of them carried pepper spray and at least one other had a Taser, the kind with ejectable prongs. Yeah. They'd be okay. And so he let her go.

Just one night, but God help him, he'd begun to want two.

Colt's smiling face was the first thing to greet him as he pulled in to the ranch, something that surprised him. It was close to midnight. The Galloping Girlz trailer was parked alongside the hay barn, which made Chance feel moderately better. Carolina had made it home safely. The apartment above the barn was dark, however. She must have returned home well ahead of him and already gone to bed. He didn't want to think about what she might look like in that bed. It would do crazy things to his insides.

"Welcome back," his brother said.

"What are you doing up?"

Sage and fresh-cut grass. That's what it smelled like when he stepped out of the truck.

Home.

"Couldn't sleep," his brother answered.

Colt headed straight for the back of the trailer. Teddy needed to be unloaded. Chance would take the panels off the trailer tomorrow. Too tired and too dark tonight.

"Word on the street is your first solo performance went off without a hitch."

Chance smiled. "Went as well as could be expected." Strangely, he didn't want to let his brother know how much he had enjoyed it. "Still wish you could have been there."

"Nah. I needed to stay here, just in case. I knew you'd be fine."

Hard to believe B day was right around the corner, as

he'd been calling it. Birth of his brother's baby. "Natalie okay?"

"She's fine. Now tell me what you thought. Did you like it? Bill called, said you nailed it both times."

"It was good." He flipped the trailer latch up, and the bar slid free on a nearly soundless hinge. Teddy lifted his head to peer over the divider as if asking, "Who's there?"

"That's all you have to say?" his brother asked. "'It was good'?"

No. It'd been great. The most intense surge of adrenaline he'd ever had outside of jumping out of a plane, only this type of rush didn't nearly kill him. But as great as it'd been, nothing compared to his night with Caro. Nothing.

"Just tired." He stepped inside the trailer, unlatching the divider. Teddy rode untied, the horse immediately turning and unloading himself. Colt caught him by the halter.

"You mind telling me what's going on?" His brother glanced at the Galloping Girlz trailer. "Caro came home, and I had to practically pry things out of her. She headed straight to the apartment, and I haven't seen her since. And you don't seem like a man who'd just nailed his first solo performance. You miss shooting people or something?"

No. He didn't miss that at all. He missed his military family. Dusty, his best friend. Mark, his commander. He still stayed in touch with them. Still saw them when he had time to video conference, but they weren't going to be there when he went back. It was his first time thinking about that, and it put a new perspective on things. It wasn't that he needed their camaraderie. He'd make new friends. It was just that things wouldn't be the same.

"I'm out of sorts," Chance admitted.

He and Colt had always been close. They'd looked out for each other when they were younger. When they were old enough, they'd turned their attention to Claire, protecting her, making sure she was okay when their dad fell into one of his drunken rages. They might be older now, but they were still close despite Chance's longer stint in the army.

"You know," Colt said, "you don't have to leave."

They'd reached Teddy's corral, Chance pausing for a moment outside the horse's pen to glance back at his brother. He rested a hand on the top rail.

"I know," he said, unbuckling Teddy's halter. One would think the horse would be tired after the long ride, but the gelding shot off, bucking, running and shaking his head until he hit the middle of his pen, where he stopped and sniffed the ground. Chance knew what would come next. Sure enough, the horse carefully lowered himself down, then rolled with joyful grunts and flailing legs. Chance couldn't help but smile.

"You could take over Rodeo Misfits, you know," his brother added. "Permanently."

Chance immediately shook his head. "Nah. Not for me."

"No, wait," Colt said. "Hear me out."

They both leaned against the fence. Chance could barely make out his brother's face, but he could tell by his voice that this was one of those serious moments in life. They'd had a few of them over the years. When their dad was sick. When they'd signed up for the army. The day Claire turned three and Colt had pulled Chance aside and sworn to protect her. He'd been five years old at the time, and he still remembered it like yesterday.

"Natalie would never want me to give up Rodeo Misfits," Colt said. "It's part of her life. But we're crazy busy right now. It's all I can do to keep up with the work around here. We have Laney to help, but it's not enough. There are horse shows and clinics and big international competitions coming up. Rodeo Misfits needs to take a backseat, but I hate to do that. It's a family business, one that was started by our grandfather."

"I know."

Colt continued as if he hadn't spoken. "Our dad nearly ruined its reputation. It's taken me years to get it back. I hate to let it all go while I go on hiatus, so why don't you take it over for me?"

"Colt—"

"Ah, ah. Don't talk." His brother lifted a hand. "You can go back to private contracting at any point in your life. And I don't want to give up the rodeo business if I don't have to. I just need a little bit of time. You can give me that, right? Stick around for a while. Live in the apartment if you want. Or build your own place. I know you've always wanted to do that out by the pond. Go for it. This land is as much yours as it is mine and Claire's."

"Can I talk now?"

His brother nodded. "Sure."

"I'm not going to lie. I really liked performing in front of a crowd."

Colt lifted up on his heels. "I *knew* it."

"And I could see how it might get addicting."

"The best high in the world."

"But I have a plan. Back to the Middle East. Make a ton of money. Save up for the house I want to build."

"You could make a ton of money performing."

"That's your money."

Colt shook his head. "No, it's not. It's our money. Our family. Our life. Don't turn your back on it."

"I'm not."

"And you're good at performing. And you won't get killed doing it. I hate the thought of you leaving and going back."

"Colt—" He sighed.

"No, let me finish. Things are good here. Claire is happy. Adam is getting better. You should be a part of that happiness."

"I am."

Colt grunted. "Vicariously."

"I keep tabs on all of you."

"Through the internet."

Chance smiled. "It works."

"It's a cop-out."

He winced. "Ouch."

"You're running away. Again. Even Caro agrees."

"What?"

"I talked to her about it earlier. Asked what she thought of you sticking around. She said you were a natural. That once you got in front of the audience you came to life." Colt shook his head. "She said it was cool to watch."

She thought he was good? During all their time together last night, she'd never once brought it up.

"You two okay?" Colt asked. "She seemed a little strange when I asked about you."

He almost laughed. *I'll bet.*

"We're fine." And that's all he would say about that. "Look, I'll think about it," Chance said before Colt asked any more probing questions. "It's been a long day. Honestly, I'm too tired to think."

But he wouldn't take over the Rodeo Misfits. He'd made a commitment to his new employer, Jax Stone. He would honor it. He always did.

"I guess that's all I can hope for." Colt frowned, and Chance suspected his brother knew the truth. "We want you here, bro. All of us do."

Chance's gaze snagged on the apartment window above the barn.

All?

CARO SHOT BACK from the glass. Had he seen her? What had they been talking about? Had Chance told Colt about their night together? Was Chance even thinking about her?

He'd looked up.

So, yes, she'd been on his mind. Or maybe he'd sensed her gaze. She'd gone from being stalked to the one doing the stalking. Stupid woman.

Inga's nails clicked against the hardwood floors as she made her way back to her couch. There was a bed in the apartment, but she refused to sleep in it. It wasn't hers and never would be. Two people had lived there— she would make it three—but none of them permanently, so there was a hodgepodge of old furniture, mostly rejects from the old house, but the furniture all worked together somehow. She would love to find someplace just like it…eventually. When life settled back to normal.

Normal. Hah. "I knew what I was getting into, didn't I, Inga?"

The Belgian Malinois rested her head against the edge of the couch while Caro buried herself under the blankets. She'd watched Chance pull in, hadn't known Colt was in the barn until she'd watched him walk up to his brother. A part of her had been disappointed—she'd been hoping Chance would come up to the apartment, but she knew that wouldn't happen with his brother watching.

He still could come up, though. Later.

Her heart began to pound just as it had when he first pulled in. He hadn't said a word to her when she'd left, but she'd seen the look in his eyes. He'd watched her walk away with an unmistakable glint. The heat of a man who'd had the time of his life and wanted more. His look had buoyed her spirits for the rest of the day. She'd been hoping it'd meant something. That he wouldn't simply let her end it.

The silence of the night was almost unbearable.

Carolina waited, breathless, for him to arrive. Colt had to have gone back to bed. Chance could easily sneak out. A horse banged against a stall, and she about came off the couch. Inga whined. She glanced at her cell phone. An hour had gone by.

Chance wasn't coming.

How long she waited for him she had no idea, but eventually she drifted off to sleep, waking only when her alarm sounded early the next morning.

He hadn't come.

She sat up in bed, Inga catching her eye. Caro mustered a smile for the dog.

"I'm a fool, aren't I?"

She tried to keep her disappointment at bay. It wasn't as if they were a couple. She'd made it clear she understood the rules. She'd just hoped he might break them.

Maybe he'd be up, too. She'd set her alarm for 5 a.m. so she could help out with feeding the animals—her way of helping to pay the rent, so to speak. The thought that Chance might be below her in the barn prompted her to dress quickly. Sweatshirt and jeans, her typical morning attire. Hardly glamorous, but she did brush her hair and apply a layer of lip gloss before heading downstairs.

BITCH.

Caro froze.

It was one of those moments when your eyes see something in front of them, but your brain can't process the information.

SLUT.

WHORE.

The words were sprayed everywhere. Stall fronts. The office door. The wall of the tack room.

"Son of a—"

The Reynolds's beautiful barn. Ruined. Because of her.

The horses.

She raced to the first stall. The animal seemed fine. So did the next one. And the next. But the barn. Caro's eyes filled with tears, humiliating, shameful, saddened tears. This was *her* fault. *Her* problem with James. *Her* mess to clean up.

"What the—"

Caro jumped, but it was Colt, not Chance, who stood near the barn's entrance. When she spotted the horrified expression on her boss's face, she couldn't hold back the tears.

She inhaled deeply and forced out the words, "I'm so sorry," before losing it completely and covering her face with her hands.

Damn him, she thought. *Damn that James Edwards.* This was the final straw. Somehow, she'd make him pay. She needed to figure out how.

Chapter Nineteen

"What a mess."

"Shh," Natalie hissed, glancing in Caro's direction. "She'll hear you." She shook her head, scrubbing the paint off the front of a stall as best she could given her ever-expanding girth. "She feels bad enough as it is."

The stall fronts were wood. They'd been stained a natural gold, and fortunately for Natalie and Colt, they were waterproof. The paint didn't stick to the surface well, which meant a rag and solvent would wipe away the paint. Unfortunately, the solvent smelled horrible, and the paint made a mess of the rags and their hands.

"What did Chance say?" Claire asked, working on getting rid of the letter *W*. Adam had insisted on helping, though she wasn't certain he should be reading the offensive words. Fortunately, he didn't know what any of them meant.

"He would kill him," Natalie said.

"You mean James." Claire rubbed a little harder. Right now she wanted to kill him, too.

"Yes, James. I also think Colt wants to kill him." Natalie worked on an *H*, but she made slow progress because she couldn't put her back into it.

Claire wouldn't be surprised if she had the baby a

little early. She'd dropped in the past week, an observation she kept to herself. She had a feeling her sister-in-law was a bit nervous. Not that she blamed her. First children were always a little terrifying.

"Mommy, what's a whore?"

Natalie gaped. Claire almost laughed. She glanced at Caro, who clearly hadn't heard the question—she was too busy working on the word *SLUT*.

"It's someone who likes men," she improvised.

"A lot of men," Natalie muttered.

"Are you a whore then, Mommy?"

Natalie and Claire exchanged glances. They both burst out laughing.

"No, honey," she chortled. "I'm not a whore."

"But you like men?" There was such a look of wide-eyed innocence on Adam's face that it somehow made it all the funnier.

"I do, but I'll explain it to you later."

"Okay," said her son, the curiosity in his green eyes fading before he went back to work.

Please, God, don't let him ask his teacher what the word meant. That would be just her luck. Although she wouldn't complain. Adam had recently gone back to normal school, as he liked to call it, and she was beyond pleased. He was thriving.

Only a few weeks until Christmas. They were marking each day on the calendar. Only a few weeks until he was deemed cancer free.

"He's going to get an education helping us clean up," Natalie said with a glance at the word *BITCH*.

"We're in luck. He knows that's a female dog."

Natalie smiled. "Thank God for that." She continued scrubbing. "And thank God all the words are short."

"Yeah, it's too bad the men aren't here to help." She smiled at her sister-in-law before rolling her eyes. "I'd like to see my brother come up with a PC explanation for what a whore is."

"Me, too," Natalie said.

They'd gone to town to talk to Officer Connelly. All of the men. There was no proof it was James they'd caught on videotape spray painting the walls, but they all knew it was. The man had worn a ski mask and baggy pants. Chance and Colt were trying to see what they could do about it, but Claire had a feeling she knew the answer. Nothing.

"Okay, that word's gone," Caro said, coming up behind them.

"Good. You can get started on *BITCH*," Natalie said.

Caro didn't immediately move off. "I'm sorry about this, Natalie. I really am."

Natalie paused, rested a hand on her giant belly. "I told you it's okay."

"I know, but I still feel bad."

Claire could tell her sister-in-law empathized. Claire felt bad for her, too.

"Not to worry," Natalie said, going back to scrubbing, her free hand resting on her belly. "We'll be done in a flash with all of us working together."

Caro turned away, clearly with the intention of helping Adam next, but she stopped. "What did you say?"

Claire paused, too, wondering what was up.

"I said it'll go fast since we're such a big group," Natalie repeated. "Fortunately, the paint is not staining the wood. Thank God for a good water sealant."

Caro had a blank stare on her face. She half turned

toward the entrance of the barn. "I wonder if that would work?"

"How what would work?" Claire asked, because clearly her sister-in-law hadn't noticed the expression on Caro's face. She wasn't talking about the paint.

"A group of us," Caro said.

"Doing what?"

"Confronting James."

Natalie understood at last. "You're going to confront him?" She glanced at Claire.

Caro nodded. "Those women. They dropped the charges against him. They were too afraid. But there's safety in numbers."

Claire nodded, supporting the idea. It could work.

"I need to call Officer Connelly," Caro said, smiling for the first time today. "I'm going to see if he'll work with me to contact the other women. Maybe if I can convince them to reopen their cases, James will leave me alone."

"You want to *what*?"

It was the first time she'd spoken to Chance all day, and it wasn't to talk about what had happened between them. Instead she'd come to him with a harebrained idea of confronting James.

"I already talked to Officer Connelly," Caro said. "He couldn't tell me who the other women were, but he promised to talk to them to see if they'd go along with my plan. If they do, Officer Connelly will break the news to James. Leave me alone or he'll have two other women pressing charges. That would be three strikes. That should scare the you-know-what out of him."

They were outside, Chance having just come from

town, the sun so bright it turned Caro's eyes a neon blue. He admired the effect for a moment before focusing on her words.

"So you're hoping to threaten him? Is that it?"

She nodded. "More or less. Leave me alone or more troubles will come your way."

"And if the other women don't play along?"

For the first time, she lost some of her enthusiasm. "Then I'll try it without their knowing. Lie if I have to, though I'd really hate that."

He'd rather drag the man out behind their barn and cut the rope right when they got near a cliff. It was bad enough James terrorized Caro, but now he'd targeted his family. The man needed to pay.

"No way, Caro. I say you keep a low profile until your first court appearance. No more rodeos. No more going out unless you absolutely have to. I've already talked to my sister about using one of her dogs for protection. You already have Inga, so I know James won't get too close. A few canine razor blades ought to put the fear of God into the man. Frankly, I'd like to stand by and watch."

"Stay home?" Her face paled. "And give up rodeos?"

"Temporarily," Chance said, hating the look on her face. He hated all of this. Nobody was allowed to mess with the people he loved.

Loved?

The people he cared for, he quickly amended.

"But trick riding is my job."

"I know that, and I already talked to Colt about it. He's going to hire you to work on the ranch with him. You'll be earning money and staying out of James's reach at the same time."

And staying away from him. He couldn't help but think that might be for the better. When he'd spied James's handiwork this morning, he'd experienced such a huge surge of rage it'd scared the hell out of him. He'd wanted to track James down—a skill he possessed and one he could use to his advantage if need be—but he hadn't trusted what he might do to the man. Compounding Chance's rage was the knowledge it'd been partly his fault James had gotten so close. He'd been exhausted from his night with Caro and the long drive home. He'd been off his game. He should have heard James outside—should have seen him. Chance hadn't, and it enraged him all the more. Colt had talked him down, but the whole thing had been a slap in the face.

"They've already been so kind to me," Caro said softly. "First with the apartment, and now this." Her blue eyes were troubled. She fingered the strands of her ponytail absently. "I don't think I can accept their offer."

"You can, because we'd all rather you be safe than sorry."

"Yeah, but there's a fine line between being a victim and a mooch."

"You're not a mooch."

"I'm still going to wait until I hear back from Officer Connelly."

She tipped her chin up, and he almost smiled. Bully for her. Instead of moping about her situation or getting angry, she'd devised a plan. The urge to kiss her right then was so surprising and so unexpected he took a step back.

"Keep me posted."

Her blue eyes lost their luster. "I will."

He couldn't get away from her fast enough, and that should have been his first clue their one night wasn't enough. His second clue came that night when she texted him.

Heard from Officer Connelly. The other two women won't do it.

And he finally understood what it meant to feel sympathy pangs. His stomach twisted in a knot at her words. She might not be in front of him, but he could practically hear her disappointment, sadness and regret.

I'm sorry, he texted back.

I guess I'm grounded.

He hated James more in that moment. It wasn't right he could affect her like this. He shouldn't be able to terrorize women and get away with it.

Especially when one of those women was his.

Chance might as well admit it. He would always despise the man for what he'd done to Caro, but something had changed.

Nobody was allowed to hurt someone who was his. Not now. Not when he'd been a kid. Not when he'd been in the army.

The man was going down. Chance simply needed to figure out how he was going to do it.

Chapter Twenty

She stayed home the next weekend, and she hated it.

It'd been one of the hardest things in her life to watch Chance leave without her. Her teammates had waved goodbye, too.

"Not easy, is it?" Colt said, turning to her as they stood in front of the barn.

"No."

He patted her back. "You'll get back to it soon enough."

Maybe.

The rodeo season would end soon. Chance would be gone. Nothing would be the same again.

"Come on." He gave her a wry grin. "Let's muck stalls."

So she kept herself busy. Inga kept her company. That helped, but only so much. Officer Connelly had called to say they'd moved up James's court date. It was the best he could do, he'd told her. He'd also said to be extra careful. There was no telling what James was capable of. His scare tactics hadn't worked, and that might make him desperate enough to try something else.

Carolina didn't see Chance when he returned from the rodeo. He had a meeting about his new job. It served as a crushing reminder he'd be gone soon. She had heard from Delilah that things had gone well at the rodeo. Delilah had stepped in and taken her place again, something her friend had only been too happy to do. And Caro knew why: Delilah had a crush on Chance.

"What should I do next?" she asked her boss, stowing away the pitchfork she'd been using to muck stalls.

Colt glanced at the whiteboard hanging on the tack-room wall. It was Monday. No clients at the barn. That meant a quiet day, something Caro could use. Her hands hadn't stopped shaking since she'd heard James was going to court.

"Why don't you lunge Titan next?" Colt suggested, tipping his cowboy hat back. "You can use the covered arena."

She nodded and gave him a faux salute, another thing that reminded her of Chance. "Will do."

At least she got to work with horses. If she were to be a prisoner for an undetermined length of time, it helped that her job dealt with the animals she loved.

"Colt," someone called.

Caro froze. Her boss turned toward the barn entrance. Natalie stood with an amused look on her face.

"It's time," she said.

Chance dropped the lead rope he'd been holding. "Right now?"

Natalie rolled her eyes. "No. Ten minutes from now. Yes, right now."

Caro glanced between them, her mind spinning. "I'll put Inga away," she said, whistling for her dog. She'd gone off to explore the manure pile, a favorite hangout for the ranch animals. "And the horses we have in turnout." Her boss's look of bemused terror amused the heck out of her, too. "I can follow behind in a few minutes."

"No," he said. "We'll wait for you."

"I don't think that's a good idea," Natalie said, wincing. "Oh, Lord."

Colt ran for his wife, calling over his shoulder, "Okay, follow behind."

And they were gone. Caro called Inga to her side. The dog had become her constant companion. "Natalie's going to have a baby," she told her. "That means you need to stay home."

Home.

She wished the ranch were her home. She'd never felt so safe. So protected. So loved as she had staying with the Reynoldses. Chance might have been keeping his distance, but that was to be expected. They'd had a deal, she and him. She didn't blame him for honoring it. She just…missed him. She missed their practice sessions. She missed how overprotective he was. She missed being made to feel as if she were special when she nailed a routine and he smiled at her in approval.

Carolina drove to the hospital in a near daze. The only thing she made a conscious decision about was to double back in case James followed her. She didn't see him, and she was in too much of a hurry to get to the hospital to do it again.

And that's why she didn't spot him in the hospital parking lot, waiting for her to get out of the truck.

"Hello, Caro."

She pressed her back up against the vehicle. They were in a crowded parking lot. People came and went. She heard an ambulance in the distance.

He's not going to hurt you here.

She did something she would have been unable to do two months ago. She squared her shoulders and stepped forward.

"Hello, James."

Lord, what had she seen in the man?

She'd found his loosely cropped brown hair attractive when she'd first met him. Now she loathed its contrived messiness. She'd liked his gray eyes, too. Had thought them kind. Now she knew they hid the soul of an evil man.

"We need to talk," he said.

"How did you know I'd be here?" she asked, her heart rate suddenly taking off.

He glanced around. Someone parked their car a few rows away. "I followed Colt and Natalie. Once I realized where they were going, I knew you wouldn't be far behind."

"Oh." Clever. She should have taken better precautions. If she hadn't been mooning over Chance, she might have noticed James waiting for her.

"I want you to drop the charges," he said, crossing big arms over his chest. "I don't need the grief a conviction will bring me."

She almost laughed. He didn't need the grief? Had she needed the bruises he'd given her? The trip to the hospital? The succeeding weeks of pain, sadness and fear?

She stood strong. "I guess you should have thought of that when you beat the crap out of me."

He took one step toward her. They were in the middle of a parking aisle, she reminded herself. She could run if she had to. Duck behind one of the other vehicles. Call for help.

"I don't think you understand. I really need you to drop those charges."

There was menace in his eyes. She didn't care. The man was a bully. She would not allow him to bully her again.

"Is that what your graffiti at my work was all about? A pep talk? A way to woo my sympathies?" She curled her lip at him, hoping he could see her complete disdain. "Get a life, James. And get a good lawyer. You're going down."

She turned away, focusing on the two-story hospital in front of her. They had security inside. She just needed to make it to the lobby.

BOOM.

The sound made her jump and turn and scream all at the same time. James stood by her truck. He held a baseball bat, though where he'd gotten it from was anyone's guess. And her truck—it now sported a huge dent in the tailgate.

James swung the bat again, this time at her taillight.

"What are you doing?" Plastic shattered. "You're ruining my truck!"

"Drop the charges," he ordered.

"Drop dead," she said, backing away from him, the hairs on her neck standing on end. He would kill her with that bat.

She ran.

Right into a wall. Only it wasn't a wall. It was Chance, and she wanted to cry, wanted to hold him tight, wanted to take shelter in his arms and never leave his side.

Never.

"LEAVE HER THE hell alone," Chance told James, hating the man more than he'd ever hated someone or something in his life.

"Screw off, asshole," James said, waving the baseball bat in their direction.

It was all Chance could do not to thrust Caro aside. To launch at the man and use the bat to pummel some sense into him. Instead he said, "If you don't leave her alone, you'll regret it."

James cocked a brow at him, slapping the bat into the palm of his hand. "Oh, yeah? Whatcha gonna do? File a restraining order against me? Big strong Army Ranger needs a piece of paper to protect him?"

He had no idea how the man knew he was ex-military, nor did he care. "No. I paid a visit to Rose Santos and Carla Brown and told them I was with a special-victims unit. I showed them pictures of what you'd done to Caro."

The memory turned his stomach all over again. His hands shook. He clenched them to avoid wrapping them around James's throat.

"I told them what you were doing to Caro, what you would do to other women if they didn't all band together to stop you." He unclenched his hands, keeping a wary eye on the baseball bat. "And you know what, James? They agreed. They put aside their fear and their terror and their revulsion of you, and they agreed to refile charges. As we speak, Officer Connelly has a warrant out for your arrest. In fact, he's right over there—" he pointed to the right "—along with several of his officers. We all saw you pull up in front of the hospital."

Caro's eyes filled with tears, but they weren't tears of fear. They were tears of joy, relief and, yes, gratitude.

He hugged her tighter before setting her aside, putting himself between her and James.

James had lost his cocky self-assurance. He glanced around him, wide-eyed. Three officers approached, guns drawn.

"Drop the weapon," one of them shouted.

Chance saw it then. Saw the fear he'd been hoping to see. The desire to run. The panic. All the things James had made his victims feel.

Chance laughed. "And here's something funny—my sister-in-law isn't having a baby right now, asshole. This was all a setup. You're going down, and I'm the man who made it happen."

Chapter Twenty-One

They put him in jail.

"But how did you know he would follow Colt and Natalie to the hospital?" Caro asked Chance. They all sat around the kitchen table: Claire, Natalie, Colt and Chance. Adam was in the family room playing video games. Inga and Natalie's new puppy kept him company.

"We didn't," Natalie answered for him. "We just knew he'd been watching the place, so we figured he'd follow us, thinking you were in the truck."

Chance nodded his agreement, which was all he'd been doing since they'd arrived home. He'd been as quiet as a possum.

"I still can't believe you didn't tell me about this," Colt said. "I thought for sure you were having that baby."

Caro glanced at Natalie in time to see her smile. "We needed to make sure Caro thought it was real."

"And I needed to draw James out," Chance said, his first words since they'd returned to the ranch. "My biggest concern was he might bring a weapon." His gaze encompassed the whole table. "A real weapon. I was glad to see all he had was a baseball bat. Even better, it's all on the hospital's security cameras. Between Carla and

Rose pressing charges and the video, James will go away for a long, long time."

Caro wanted to cry. It was over. Chance had done it. He'd saved her as he'd saved so many people over the course of his life.

"Thank you," she said softly.

He glanced at her, but she couldn't read the expression in his eyes and it drove her nuts. She would have thought he'd be ecstatic, but instead he'd been quiet, almost sad.

"Well, I still think you should have told me," Colt said, getting up and filling a glass with water at the tap. "I drove like a maniac on our way to the hospital."

"You'll get to drive like a maniac again," Natalie said, standing, too.

She doubled over.

"Nat!" Colt yelled, the glass clattering in the sink.

"It's okay," she wheezed. She lifted a hand. "Just knocked the breath out of me."

"What?" Colt asked.

Natalie peeked up at him. "I think I had my first contraction."

Claire gaped. "You're in labor?"

She grunted, leaned over again, managing to gasp. "We need to get back to the hospital."

From the family room, they heard Adam say, "Again?"

Which made Natalie and Colt laugh. Caro looked at Chance, wanting to ask him what was wrong. He should be excited. He was about to become an uncle again. But as she watched, he stood without saying a word. He grabbed his hat and shoved it on his head.

"I'll drive me and Caro to the hospital."

Her relief was like a physical release. She could feel

her shoulders relax. He wouldn't be able to ignore her in the truck.

"I'll put the dogs away first," she volunteered.

"We'll ride with Colt and Natalie," Claire said, turning to the family room. "Come on, Adam."

The boy sighed in resignation as Caro scooped up the puppy. It took her only a minute to lock the baby Malinois in the laundry room and another few minutes to lock up Inga.

Shortly after, she climbed into the truck beside Chance.

"Seat belt," he reminded her.

He didn't smile. Didn't comment on his sister-in-law's impending delivery. Didn't do anything other than stare straight ahead and put the truck in drive.

"Chance, what's wrong?"

She thought he would ignore her. Thought he might brush her off with a comment. Instead he shifted in his seat, glancing at her for a second.

"I'm leaving in a couple weeks."

The words were like the stab of a needle. No, a hundred needles…a thousand. She'd known it was coming. She'd never deluded herself into thinking it wasn't. Still…

"I'm sorry to hear that," she said, looking out the passenger-side window. She didn't want him to see her eyes. If he did, he might note the tears she fought.

"I heard from my new commander over the weekend. I fly out to Germany first, then back to the Middle East."

Back to the war zone. A place where he might be killed. A place of danger.

She gulped down the lump in her throat. "What will you do there?"

He shrugged. "Mostly escorting corporate executives in and around war zones."

She nodded, her voice raspy with unshed tears as she asked, "Isn't that dangerous?"

He shrugged again. "I'm used to danger."

Yes, he was. She could not have asked for a better bodyguard. It was what he did. What he was good at. She didn't blame him for wanting to go back to it.

But was it wrong of her to wish? To dream? To wonder what might have happened had she been woman enough to capture his heart? She inhaled against more tears.

"Congratulations?" She forced a bright smile, making sure she had herself firmly in control before turning to face him. "I think."

At last their gazes met, and Caro's heart flipped over at what she saw. Sadness. Resignation. Maybe even a hint of fear. But no. Chance didn't feel fear. He was a warrior. A man who had dedicated his life to protecting people, no matter what it might cost him personally.

"No, it's good." He focused on the road again. "I'm going to break the news to Colt and Natalie once the baby is born."

Good Lord, it was getting hard to breathe. "And the rodeo business? What about that?"

He gripped the steering wheel, hard. "It's almost the end of the season. And I won't be leaving for a little while yet. I'll be able to finish it out."

Leaving. She'd known it was coming. Still…

"Take care of yourself while you're over there," she said. "Promise me you'll keep in touch."

They'd reached the end of the ranch's private road, and Chance held her gaze as he said, "I will."

IT WAS THE longest night of his life, not because his brother's wife was in labor for twelve hours before she finally gave birth to a healthy baby boy they named Weston, but because he kept catching glimpses of Caro's face while they waited all afternoon for news.

Her face was splotchy. Pinched. Dark circles rimmed her eyes.

He wasn't an idiot. He knew why she'd barely cracked a smile when the Galloping Girlz arrived at the hospital. One of them had asked her if everything was okay. He'd watched as she'd pasted on a bright smile and explained she was just tired now that everything was over with James.

Don't think about it, buddy. This was always the deal.

He knew that. Just as she'd known it, too. Didn't make it any easier to swallow, because the plain and simple truth was he cared. If things had been different, he would have asked her out. He would have wooed and wined and dined her and...

What?

No sense in dwelling on what wouldn't ever happen.

"You can go in now," a nurse said, her smile aimed at the lobby of waiting people. All of Colt and Natalie's friends. Wes and Jillian. Zach and Mariah. Ethan, his sister's fiancé. "Just close family for now."

He stood. Ethan and Claire did, too, his sister holding out her hand for Adam. Caro stayed seated, but Chance motioned her up. "You're part of the family, too."

He caught the look of surprise on his sister's face, but she didn't balk. Claire was too sweet for that, and Natalie didn't seem to mind when they came in together. In fact, she smiled brightly.

"Look what the stork brought."

Adam rushed to the bed, most likely because he couldn't see the baby swaddled in blankets, but when he finally caught his first glimpse, he drew up short.

"Why is he so red?"

There was such a look of intrigued revulsion on the boy's face that Chance would have laughed if he'd been in a better frame of mind.

"He's exhausted," Natalie said, her eyes as blue as the blankets around her son. "It's a lot of work being carried by a stork all that way."

To which Adam replied, "Aunt Natalie, I know babies don't come from a stork. They come from vaginas."

Stunned silence. Colt emitted a sound reminiscent of a bird squawking. Natalie glanced at Claire. Claire shrugged. Then, as if on cue, they all started laughing. Caro just watched, and Chance realized she felt like an intruder. He scooted closer to her and whispered, "My nephew has no filter."

She glanced up at him and smiled gratefully. "So I've learned."

"What do you think, you guys?" Natalie said, holding her baby differently to give everyone a better view. "Weston, meet your family. Family, meet Weston."

Meet your family.

"I think he's adorable," his sister said.

"I think he looks like a dried-up tomato." Adam chortled.

"And I think he's perfect," his soon-to-be brother-in-law said. "I want one just like him."

Which made Claire look at Ethan with adoration. Chance averted his gaze. He knew now why he'd invited Caro into the room. He felt like an outsider, too. The brother who had always been off on another continent. The one who only saw people via video chat and conversed through text messages. It had never bothered him before, but right now it did. In a couple of weeks, he'd be leaving. Life would go on here. Ethan was talking about starting up a therapy center for veterans suffering from PTSD. He didn't have the money to do it himself, so Chance had connected him with a wealthy friend—the man he was going to work for, actually, Jaxston Stone, the owner of DTS.

"How are you feeling, Natalie?" Caro asked. Hospital lights did nothing to detract from her pretty features. Chance longed to touch her face.

Natalie smiled. "Tired. Sore. Elated. Scared."

"Scared?" Caro asked.

She glanced around the room with a bemused expression on her face. "It occurred to me a few minutes ago that this little bundle of joy is now solely my responsibility."

"And mine," Colt added.

"Yes, but still a responsibility. It's like learning you were given a monkey."

"A monkey!" Colt said. "Are you calling my son ugly?"

"He kind of looks like a monkey," Adam said.

Natalie smiled again. "No, no. I'm just saying that monkeys are cute, and I think I might know how to care for one, but until I do, it's a little scary."

"I know exactly how you feel," Claire said. "But you'll get used to it. In a few years, you'll be missing the days when he couldn't talk back."

"Can I hold him?" Adam interjected.

"Of course," Natalie said. "Just make sure you support his head."

They all watched as the two cousins were introduced to each other, and Chance found himself wanting to slip an arm about Caro and draw her closer. It must be the emotions of the day that had him feeling so out of sorts.

"You want to hold him, Chance?" Natalie asked, motioning with her chin toward Adam. "You'll be leaving us here soon. Better get your fill."

He gulped. Did he want to hold his nephew? He hadn't been around for Adam's birth. Come to think of it, he couldn't recall a single time that he'd held an infant.

"Ah, sure?"

Adam turned to him. "It's easy. Just don't break his head."

Chance almost laughed. Almost. Because in the next instant, he was holding his nephew and staring down into his eyes and he saw... Colt. And his sister. And his mother before that, and it reminded him of his mom and how much he missed her, and how he wished she were here right now. He needed to look away, because the man who didn't cry, who prided himself on never shedding tears, suddenly couldn't breathe.

Something was wrong.

The whole way home Chance said not one word. She'd tried to engage him in conversation, but he'd merely grunted a time or two. She'd given up after the first few miles.

"See you this weekend," he said as he put his truck in gear. He moved to open his door.

"Chance." She stopped him with her hand.

He reacted as if she'd hit him. It immediately prompted her to pull her hand away.

"Sorry," she said, though she didn't know why she

was apologizing. "I wanted to say I don't want things to be awkward between us. We still have two more rodeos to perform together. I want them to be good times, not bad."

Night had fallen, but she could still make out his face in the light of the dashboard.

"I'm going to miss my family," he said.

She reached for him again. It was an automatic gesture, and this time he didn't pull away. This time he let her hand rest on his.

"I looked around the hospital room, and I realized I would be gone soon, but they would still be here, back at the ranch, living life without me."

Don't go.

Oh, how she wanted to say the words.

"I won't get to see Weston grow up. Not really. I'll miss out on Adam's first prom. In a few years, they'll both be grown up and graduated and I'll be...where?"

She took a deep breath made shaky by her tears. "You'll be here," she said, her free hand lifting to her chest, "in their hearts."

He seemed so sad in that moment, so lost, that she did the unthinkable. She crossed the line, the invisible barrier that had stood between them for weeks. She kissed him. He didn't move at first, but then he kissed her back and she knew where it would lead. She didn't care.

Stay, she tried to tell him with every kiss. *Don't leave.*

He didn't seem to hear, and that was all right, too, because she was desperate enough to take what she could get. When he slipped out of his truck, she did, too. And when he held out a hand, she took it. Colt was spending the night at the hospital. They had the house to themselves. He led her to his room, his childhood bedroom, slowly undressing her, kissing her shoulder at one point.

"Did he hurt you there?" he asked.

It took her a moment to understand what he meant. "Yes."

He kissed the spot again. "I'm sorry."

It was all she could do not to cry.

I love you.

The words were right there, on the edge of her tongue, but she couldn't say them. Not when he laid her down on the bed. Not when he kissed every spot that James had bruised, including her heart. Not later, when they were done and he held her.

I love you.

If only the words would make him stay.

Chapter Twenty-Two

Chance's flight departed at three on a Sunday afternoon. Caro knew that because, unbeknownst to him, she'd driven to the airport, parked at the end of the runway and watched his plane leave the ground, tears in her eyes.

"It's for the best," she kept telling herself. The military was Chance's life. No, she quickly amended, protecting people was his life. Nothing would stop him from doing that. Not his family. Not her. Not anyone.

"You look like death," Colt said when she showed up for work. Caro had burrowed beneath a heavy sweatshirt. They'd never gone back to the way it'd been before, when all she'd done was ride for Colt on the weekends. Colt had insisted she stay on, and Caro had said yes. It beat waitressing over the winter, which was how she usually supported herself. But even she was surprised when he'd offered her the apartment as part of her salary. It was a godsend, and she knew how lucky she was.

"Just tired," she said.

"Well, get ready. You're going to be even more tired. My sister's going a little crazy with this whole wedding deal. She's already done a site map. She told me she'd be over tomorrow to figure out where they're going to put everything."

The wedding. Once it had seemed distant, far in the future, but it was only weeks away. Christmas. A time for celebrating and new beginnings. For family and friendship. She should be grateful to be included as a member of the Reynolds clan, even if she wasn't. Not really.

She had hoped.

But she refused to dwell. Losing Chance had left her numb, and she needed something, anything, to keep her occupied.

"Tell me what I can do to help," she said, forcing a smile, but her boss didn't reply. He stared down at her, concern in his eyes.

"Did you tell him you loved him?"

She thought she'd misheard him. "What?"

"My brother. Does he know you're in love with him?"

She didn't know what to say. Didn't know what to do. She could deny it, but Colt and Natalie had been so kind. She couldn't lie to them. Not now. Not ever.

"I don't think so," she said softly, looking at the ground. It was hard to look at Colt. He reminded her so much of Chance.

"You should have told him."

She took a deep breath. "I did, in a way."

Colt shook his head. "Idiot."

She didn't know if he referred to her or to Chance.

"My brother's never been one for seeing what's right in front of his face."

It was Chance he talked about, then. Phew.

"In high school, Harriet Peterson had the biggest crush on him. Everyone in school knew it, but not Chance. He was too busy riding horses, hunting squirrels or riding broncs. Clueless."

"Please don't tell him."

"I won't."

She grabbed a rake. She didn't want to talk about it anymore. It was painful enough without discussing the matter with Chance's brother.

True to his word, Colt and Claire kept her busy. The wedding promised to be a big deal with several A-list celebrities attending. Of course, Chance wouldn't be there. He'd promised to try, but since he'd just started his new job, he didn't think he'd be able to make it.

"That's my brother for you," Claire said a week before the wedding. They were in Natalie's family room, putting together wedding decorations. Caro had decided she stunk at using a glue gun, but that didn't stop her from trying to stick together twigs that would hopefully look like a tree. They planned to place the tree in the center of a table and hang tiny pictures of Claire and Ethan on the branches. "You never know when he's going to show up, or *if* he'll show up."

Caro didn't know what she would do if he did. Probably run in the other direction. Since he'd left, her feelings hadn't changed one bit, especially since he'd been true to his word. He stayed in touch. She received regular updates from him, always chatty, always upbeat, never personal. That was okay. She didn't want personal. Personal caused pain, and she'd already had enough of that in her life.

"Do you think you can get me more twigs?" Claire said. "I put a pile of them on the front stoop."

Caro nodded and headed for the front door. She was looking down, which was why she didn't immediately see him.

See *him*.

Chance.

At first, she thought she was seeing things and it was really Colt standing there. They looked so much alike. But no. It wasn't Colt. It was Chance. She couldn't breathe.

"Hello, Caro."

His voice. She'd forgotten how it sounded. So deep. So masculine. So...Chance.

"You're here." Stupid thing to say, but she couldn't think, couldn't do anything but stand stiffly.

"I'm here," he echoed.

She swallowed. "Claire will be so happy."

"Claire already knows."

Once again, she felt incapable of forming a response. "She knows?" she parroted back.

"I told her I was coming."

"But she just said—"

She straightened suddenly, realizing she'd been set up. In typical Reynolds fashion they'd orchestrated Chance's homecoming so she would walk outside right as he was arriving.

Why?

"Aren't you going to give me a kiss hello?"

And she saw it then. The crooked smile, the twinkle in his green eyes.

"Well, I don't know." She headed down the steps, stopping just in front of him. "That depends."

"On what?"

He looked so good. More tan. Fitter, if that were possible. And tired. As if he'd flown thousands of miles to be there, standing in front of her. And maybe he had.

"It depends on if you're here to stay or not." She inhaled deeply before taking the plunge. "Because I can't do it again, Chance. I can't watch you leave. The first time nearly killed me."

His Adam's apple bobbed as he swallowed. "I know."

And then he was there, in front of her, and his arms were wrapping around her and she knew it wasn't a dream. Somehow he was there and he loved her. She saw it in his eyes just before he bent his head and kissed her.

"Caro," he said softly, a long while later, drawing back and resting his chin on her head. "If only you knew how much I missed this."

Her eyes burned. She still couldn't believe it was true.

"I knew the moment my plane took off that I'd made a mistake, but I couldn't bail. I had an obligation, so I stuck it out until they could find a replacement."

She started to weep softly, because it was like a dream. A really great dream where he said all the things she'd hoped he would.

"I told them I had to be back in time for my sister's wedding because there was this girl, and she would be there and I had a question to ask her."

She ducked her head, for some reason ashamed of her tears. He tipped her head back.

"Carolina Cruthers, I love you."

She tried to duck her head again, but he wouldn't let her. Her eyes blurred with tears and she sobbed, though she tried hard not to. She wanted to see him clearly, to memorize the look in his eyes.

"I've been such a fool, Caro. I was afraid to start a new life. To let go of the familiar. To be with my real family."

His lips brushed hers. She opened eyes she hadn't known she'd closed.

"You," he said softly, gently.

And then he kissed her again and she kissed him back, letting him know without words that she loved him, and when a long while later, he stepped back and pulled a ring from his pocket, she started crying again, especially when he bent down on one knee and, in front of all the people who mattered—Claire and Ethan and Adam, Natalie and Weston and Colt, even the Galloping Girlz, who materialized out of nowhere—asked her to marry him.

"Yes," she sobbed. "Of course, yes."

He slipped the ring on her finger and then pulled her to him as she murmured, "I love you," to him for the first time in her life.

The first of many times.

Epilogue

There were three rules of a Christmas wedding. One, it must snow, even if the wedding was in California at an elevation that rarely, if ever, saw snow. Two, the bridesmaids must wear red, even if one of those bridesmaids insisted she never looked good in red, although that same bridesmaid was quite pleased with her breast-feeding boobies. Three, the bride and groom needed to arrive at the wedding in a horse-drawn wagon, jingle bells clanging, red ribbons waving, wedding guests smiling.

All three rules were honored at the wedding of Claire Reynolds and Ethan McCall. The best man, a little boy named Adam, beamed the whole time. The groomsmen, of which there were two, also beamed, although Claire's brothers insisted they outshone the bride. They maintained that brothers were allowed to tease a sister, even on that sister's wedding day.

There was another, lesser known rule: engaged couples were allowed to kiss as often as they liked. This was, perhaps, Chance Reynolds's favorite rule, and one he never broke.

"You're going to make my lips fall off," Caro teased as Chance rocked her back and forth on the dance floor.

"I swear you've kissed me more times tonight than you have the whole time we've been together."

Chance's eyes glittered. "That's because you look exceptionally beautiful tonight in your red stripper gown."

She laughed. She couldn't help it. "You better not let Claire hear you say that. She loves this color."

Her future husband smiled. "Yes, but my sister-in-law does not. I heard she might pretend to like it, but Natalie is sublimely self-aware of how it hugs her every curve. Colt said she's embarrassed."

Claire glanced in Colt and Natalie's direction. "But she looks so sexy in it."

Beneath the roof of the covered arena, which had been cleared of jumps and turned into a huge ballroom, Chance pulled her closer.

"Not as sexy as you." He lowered his head. "I swear I'm going to enjoy peeling every inch of this dress off your body tonight."

"Ah, ah, ah," she gently chided. "Not until we're married."

They'd set a date in the spring, before the start of rodeo season. Chance would be taking over his brother's business, at least for now, because ever since he'd quit working for DTS, job offers had been piling in. He was presently considering four different positions: head of security for a big internet firm; ranch manager of the soon-to-be-built Dark Horse Ranch, where veterans could be treated for PTSD and would be conveniently located next door; and her favorite, personal bodyguard to the stars. The latter offer had come in from family friend Rand Jefferson, the A-lister who'd married former Galloping Girl Samantha. But the one he was actually considering, Chance's favorite of the offers he'd received so far, was working for the sheriff's department alongside Officer Connelly. Who would have thought?

"You keep saying that," Chance said, "but I have high hopes to convince you otherwise." He wagged his eyebrows.

She playfully batted his arm. "Good luck with that, soldier."

"You guys, look!"

They both turned toward Adam, who skillfully navigated the crowded dance floor with Inga up on her hind legs. Or maybe it was Bella, Natalie's dog. It was hard to tell beneath an arena full of Christmas lights. Either way, the dog had a big red bow around her neck. She looked clearly puzzled by this new human ritual. When the dog looked into Caro's eyes, she knew it was Inga.

"Poor thing," Chance said.

Caro laughed. "She better get used to it. Once we have kids, all bets are off."

She glanced up to see the glint in his eyes. She knew he was thinking back to the day in the hospital when he'd held his nephew for the first time. She'd seen the same look on his face then. Longing. Happiness. Belonging.

"Soon enough," she said softly.

"Yes. Soon," he echoed, because they weren't going to wait. Once they were married, they would try to get pregnant right away. Caro vowed that she would bring their children up in a completely different way than her own upbringing. Chance had vowed the same thing. Perhaps between the two of them, two previously damaged people could make good parents. She knew they would.

He kissed her again, and she didn't have the heart to tease him anymore. She loved him. Heart and soul. She didn't know what she'd done to deserve him, but now that she had him, she would never let him go.

"Hey, hey," said the bride as she danced by on her groom's arm, her smile bright enough to light the room. "Save it for later."

Ethan laughed gently as he whisked Claire by the two of them. Colt and Natalie twirled by next, Colt pasting a lascivious grin on his face as he pretended to gawk at his wife's magnificent cleavage. Everyone laughed. Caro and Chance. Samantha and her famous husband, Rand. Wes and Jillian. Mariah and Zach. So many friends. So much love in the room. Caro didn't think her heart could ever be as full.

Once upon a time, she'd dreamed of being part of the Reynolds family. Back then she would have never imagined that her dream could come true. So many things had gone wrong in her life, starting with her childhood and ending with James. But one thing had gone right, and it was the most important thing. She'd found the man of her dreams.

Three months later, as she and Chance said their wedding vows, Carolina knew a joy like no other. It was a day of celebration. Adam had been officially declared cancer free. Claire and Ethan had learned they were pregnant, a feat Chance vowed to replicate, soon.

And as they danced at their own wedding, this time by the pond that was really more like a lake, in the spot where Chance had declared he would build his own small family a home, Caro realized she'd been wrong.

It was possible to feel as if your heart might burst with love. That same feeling could happen again and again. And it did. Through the birth of children, more weddings, more children and all the things that life brought the two of them. And though their lives were full of the inevitable ups and downs, they loved each other.

And that was the most important rule of all.

* * * * *

#1601 A TEXAS SOLDIER'S FAMILY
Texas Legacies: The Lockharts
by Cathy Gillen Thacker

PR expert Hope Winslow has just taken on a big Dallas scandal. Garrett Lockhart is summoned home to help protect his family name. But who will protect him from falling for Hope and her adorable infant son?

#1602 A RANCHER TO LOVE
Blue Falls, Texas • by Trish Milburn

Leah Murphy moves to Tyler Lowe's ranch hoping to find peace. She is drawn to the single rancher as he looks after his five-year-old niece. But can Leah trust a man again?

#1603 A MAVERICK'S HEART
Snowy Owl Ranchers • by Roz Denny Fox

When gem hunter Seth Maxwell stays at Lila Jenkins's B and B, he's not prepared for his heart to be stolen by the beautiful widow, her sweet little boy or the ranch he can imagine them sharing...

#1604 COWBOY IN CHARGE
The Hitching Post Hotel • by Barbara White Daille

Jason McAndry and Layne Slater are divorced and determined not to make the same mistake twice. But their son binds them together, and maybe love is better the second time around.

REQUEST YOUR FREE BOOKS!
2 FREE NOVELS PLUS 2 FREE GIFTS!

⬧HARLEQUIN®

American Romance®

LOVE, HOME & HAPPINESS

American Romance®

Garrett Lockhart has no idea the woman he's about to meet is someone he's about to get to know very well! The sexy military doctor is immediately entranced by Hope Winslow…and her darling baby son.

Read on for a sneak peek at
A TEXAS SOLDIER'S FAMILY
from Cathy Gillen Thacker's new
TEXAS LEGACIES: THE LOCKHARTS miniseries!

"Welcome aboard!" The flight attendant smiled. "Going home to Texas…?"

"Not voluntarily," Garrett Lockhart muttered under his breath.

It wasn't that he didn't *appreciate* spending time with his family. He did. It's just that he didn't want them weighing in on what his next step should be.

Reenlist and take the considerable promotion being offered?

Or take a civilian post that would allow him to pursue his dreams?

He had twenty-nine days to decide and an unspecified but pressing family crisis to handle in the meantime.

And an expensive-looking blonde in a white power suit who'd been sizing him up from a distance, ever since he arrived at the gate…

He'd noticed her, too. Hard not to with that gorgeous face, mane of long, silky hair brushing against her shoulders, and a smoking-hot body.

Phone to her ear, one hand trying to retract the telescoping handle of her suitcase while still managing the carryall over her shoulder, she said, "Have to go…Yes, yes. I'll call you as soon as I land in Dallas. Not to worry." She laughed softly, charmingly, while lifting her suitcase with one hand into the overhead compartment. "If you-all will just *wait* until I can—*ouch!*" He heard her stumble toward him, yelping as her expensive leather carryall crashed onto his lap.

"Let me help you," he drawled. With one hand hooked around her waist and the other around her shoulders, he lifted her quickly and skillfully to her feet, then turned and lowered her so she landed squarely in her own seat. That done, he handed her the carryall she'd inadvertently assaulted him with.

Hope knew she should say something. If only to make her later job easier.

And she would have, if the sea blue eyes she'd been staring into hadn't been so mesmerizing. She liked his hair, too. So dark and thick and…touchable…

"Ma'am?" he prodded again, less patiently.

Clearly he was expecting some response to ease the unabashed sexual tension that had sprung up between them, so she said the first thing that came into her mind. "Thank you for your assistance just now. And for your service. To our country, I mean."

His dark brow furrowed. His lips—so firm and sensual—thinned. Shoulders flexing, he studied her with breathtaking intent, then asked, "How'd you know I was in the military?"

Don't miss
A TEXAS SOLDIER'S FAMILY
by Cathy Gillen Thacker, available July 2016
everywhere Harlequin® Western Romance®
books and ebooks are sold.

www.Harlequin.com

Same great stories, new name!

In July 2016,
the HARLEQUIN®
AMERICAN ROMANCE® series
will become
the HARLEQUIN®
WESTERN ROMANCE series.

Connect with us to find your next great read,
special offers and more.

f /HarlequinBooks

🐦 @HarlequinBooks

www.HarlequinBlog.com

www.Harlequin.com/Newsletters

HARLEQUIN®

A *Romance* FOR EVERY MOOD™

www.Harlequin.com

HWR2016

Turn your love of reading into rewards you'll love with

Harlequin My Rewards

**Join for FREE today at
www.HarlequinMyRewards.com**

Earn **FREE BOOKS** of your choice.

Experience **EXCLUSIVE OFFERS** and contests.

Enjoy **BOOK RECOMMENDATIONS**
selected just for you.

PLUS! Sign up now
and get **500** points
right away!

Earn
FREE
REWARDS
Join
Today!
HarlequinMyRewards.com

MYR16R

Love the Harlequin book you just read?

Your opinion matters.

Review this book on your favorite book site, review site, blog or your own social media properties and share your opinion with other readers!

Be sure to connect with us at:
Harlequin.com/Newsletters
Facebook.com/HarlequinBooks
Twitter.com/HarlequinBooks

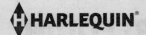

HARLEQUIN®

A *Romance* FOR EVERY MOOD™

JUST CAN'T GET ENOUGH?

Join our social communities
and talk to us online.

You will have access to the latest
news on upcoming titles and special
promotions, but most importantly,
you can talk to other fans about your
favorite Harlequin reads.

Harlequin.com/Community

Facebook.com/HarlequinBooks

Twitter.com/HarlequinBooks

Pinterest.com/HarlequinBooks

HSOCIAL